Who's On Top?

by

L. J. Martin

Print Edition

Copyright 2014 L. J. Martin

Wolfpack Publishing
48 Rock Creek Road
Clinton, Montana 59825

ISBN: 978-1-62918-293-3

Thanks

To my beautiful patient wife,
Kat Martin

To my incisive editor,
Ann LaFarge

And to my good buddy,
and brilliant associate,
Mike Bray

Chapter One

The irony of this world, and particularly of my country, oft time befuddles me.

Here I am having just finished a repairman job which took me to South America where the use of a number of firearms, including an RPG, was necessary to accomplish the recovery of a fifty million dollar G5 for a client, one of the world's finest business aircraft. Upon my return, I find I'm being hired—if I accept the assignment—by one of America's foremost anti-gun advocates. I'm sure I was not recommended to him because of my pacifist ways. And he's a guy who could afford to hire two divisions of pacifists to try and return his errant daughter. I'm on my way to the Big Apple to meet with J. Cornelius Remington. Another irony, an anti-gun advocate named...Remington.

It seems he figures words won't accomplish the recovery of the young lady. Maybe words have been tried adinfinitum...as they have, to no end, so many times in the history of the world.

I'm eager to see if Remington wants me to forgo the use of firearms, and if so, why hire me? There are plenty of bloodhound types out there who'll track someone down if someone else needs them found, and probably for far less money than I'll require. I get paid well because I take big risks, most of which involve being shot at, and if I stand the risk of being shot at, you can damn well bet I'm shooting back.

Should be an interesting meeting.

Why does my country befuddle me? The reasons would fill a book, but it's pretty well summed up by the fact that we've elected a leader who proclaims to the world that the most prosperous, productive country in the world, by multiple times, is not exceptional. Duh! Unlike others, I've always been proud of my country, even though my country, like all of her citizens, has often been wrong, mistaken, overeager, thoughtless, and lethargic. But never so much as the other countries in the world, and she's saved most of their butts from annihilation more than once. Just count the number of American boys and girls buried on foreign soil.

So, I'm on my way to meet with a guy whose name is Remington, a third generation plutocrat whose fortune is now well over a billion dollars, who's benefited almost beyond belief by the fact that the nation was founded by folks who revered personal freedom, who's benefited beyond belief by the founding document, our Constitution, and like our president, wants to change it.

Befuddled is not a strong enough word.

But if I can find a father's daughter who's gone missing I'll set my condemnation aside and do what I've always done...my job. This guy can afford to pay handsomely for the effort, and I'll enjoy taking his money.

New York is served, among other airports, by Newark Liberty International, a New Jersey airport, and that's the destination of the six AM flight I'm deplaning. Of course I've had to leave my Glock at my mini-storage—the nearest thing to a home I occupy, other than my Ford 250 and camper—but I have my mace pen which sneaks through Homeland Security and their TSA division. The last time—the only time—I was in New York City was during the Bloomberg years, and the streets were safe and fairly clean, not so much, I understand as during Giuliani's years when he drove all the panhandlers and crazies underground, but Bloomberg allowed them to creep back up and de Blasio is encouraging it. While there a short time I was, however, accosted by a couple of females with ulterior motives, and never felt the need for mace or a Glock. There are some tasks that require a different kind of weapon.

I remember New York as a fun town, although I was only there long enough to see a tiny fraction of the city.

It's good to have a close buddy—Pax Weatherwax in this instance—who's a wizard with computers, as he's produced a tome on J. Remington Printers, a one hundred fifty year old Manhattan company which, as I read, I find is now worth several billion good old not so exceptional greenbacks. Its CEO and heir to the company, founded by his great grandfather, Jasper Remington, is personally worth over a billion. The company is involved in not only printing but the manufacture of ink and paper, with operations in the U.S., Canada, and China.

A billion, and he didn't bother to send me a first class ticket so I bought my own cattle car version, next to a young man who should have been required to fly in the cargo or luggage section, or at least to have purchased two seats. He overflows into my space, but as fat guys are reputed to be, he's jolly and keeps me entertained with

11

fascinating tales of the sundries biz—the sale of advertising pens and knickknacks. Why couldn't they have seated me next to a Victoria's Secret fashion model as you would expect when flying to New York? That, of course, would require being in first class.

Newark Liberty is crawling with folks as we deplane at three PM after circling the metropolitan area for an extra half hour. As I only pack a carry on, I go straight out to public transportation and grab a bus to the city, then to my hotel, which is a place I've always wanted to stay, the Waldorf Astoria. Even the name is a class act, and although my room is not large, it manages to be very expensive. Every great once in a while I splurge, and this is one of those times. After all, I'm in the Big Apple.

It's a little after six by the time I'm settled in, so I walk over to a renowned steak house on 3rd, Smith & Wollensky, which is to my liking as it's a man's joint, with oversize portions to match its oversize prices. I take it easy on the booze with only one Jack Daniels, then one beer with my supper, return to the Waldorf and visit the Bull and Bear there, another famous joint and watering hole for my second beer, then hit the sack by eleven. It's kind of a kick to watch all the metrosexual boys with their five grand English tailored suits, five hundred buck loafers, two hundred dollar shirts and one hundred dollar ties being careful not to stain any of their outfits with meat juice or Worchestershire. All that, and I saw more than a few with four days' growth of beard…a Hollywood affectation which has spread east like a virulent flu. An affectation which I can only presume is to establish their manhood, either for their own reassurance or for attraction to whomever they may wish to bed for the night, Jim or Jane. Or at least to establish the mere fact that they possess the male gene. To my way of thinking, it's not the same thing...manhood and the possession of a male gene.

I would have thought that a prestigious company like J. Remington Printers would be located in the financial district, somewhere near Wall Street, but on inspection of the map find they are in the opposite direction, on the upper east side; too far to walk for my nine thirty appointment, so I decide to have a leisurely breakfast at Oscar's in the hotel, then cab it. As I climb in the cab, I have to laugh as I'm wondering, in my Wrangler jeans—although with a stylish crease—my open collar twenty buck Costco shirt, and my tweed sport coat with the patches on the sleeves, not to speak of my Tony Lama Ostrich boots and matching belt...will I get past the doorman? If he glances at my NRA belt buckle, I may be banned from the state.

Particularly since I've discovered that the Remington family is not only among the country's leading antigun advocates, but they're major contributors to PETA, People for the Ethical Treatment of Animals. It might have been wise to see if I could find plastic cowboy boots...now ain't that a hoot?

I'm surprised to see that the office is a five-storey brownstone which looks as if it wwere built in the mid-nineteenth century, with cast-iron columns, lions flanking a marble stairway, and a brass door befitting a major bank. And when you say 'major bank' in the Big Apple, you mean a multi-multi-billion dollar, fifty storey, edifice.

And I'm further astonished when the doorman not only welcomes me, Ostrich boots and all, but the smiling black guy who looks a little funny in a brown suit with yellow piping all nicely draped on an impressive New-

York-Giant's-tackle sized body, escorts me into a spacious room. A lovely gray haired lady, who looks as if she stepped out of the pages of Vogue, escorts me onto an elevator and even pushes the fifth floor button for me. I'm not sure if she's being doubly polite or thinks I'm so much of a country bumpkin I may not know the operation of the lift. I can't help but smile as, at least, she gives me a look from my buzz cut to my boots.

I'm wondering if the rest of the morning will be so pleasant.

Chapter Two

Another well dressed and stylishly coiffed lady meets me when the elevator doors open. This one's a redhead with eyes like emeralds, and to my admitted pleasure she's considerably younger than the first and has bumps and bulges in all the right places. She escorts me across marble floors to the outer office of J. Cornelius Remington, or so the gold letters on the door announce.

I'm asked to park it in a beautiful kid-leather-soft brown easy chair, one of a half dozen in the waiting room—marble has changed to plush wool carpet. She offers coffee or? I'd like to suggest some 'or'…but don't, and refuse, as I'm coffee'd out after a long wait at Oscar's until time to make what Manhattanites believe is an early appointment. She takes an office chair behind a walnut desk large enough to play football upon…however, eyeing her bumps and bulges as she returns to work, I can think of games I'd prefer.

I wait, absorbed in a *New Yorker* Magazine, for what seems the obligatory twenty minutes, for a man who obviously wants to prove his busy schedule. Shortly after her intercom buzzes, I'm escorted through a ten foot tall walnut door into an office with a surprisingly good view of the East River. I paused to admire the view and the layer of fog or mist sandwiched between a bright Spring sky and the busy river below—so low that the mast of a passing schooner disappears into the layer. The office is all wood, including the ceiling and flooring, with walls covered with handsomely framed prints that could be 19th century signed Audubons.

He doesn't bother to walk around the monster desk to greet me, but rather rises and offers a hand across the desk. At the same time his left hand caresses a head that's bald and liver spotted, and it's hard to tell if it's roached or the work of the years. He's a short rotund fellow not that much older than me, maybe ten years, maybe late forties. He has to bend and perch his belly on the desk to extend a hand far enough that I can reach it. It's pretty obvious he's never done a day's work with those hands as soft as a woman's. But his gaze is clear and penetrating.

"I appreciate your coming," he says, his voice closer to soprano than tenor.

"My pleasure," I reply. "I've only been in the Big Apple for a weekend a few years ago and am looking forward to seeing some of the city."

He looks a little disturbed, and sinks back into a fancy desk chair equipped with some kind of back support, and motions me to take a seat in one of two lion-footed green upholstered chairs facing him. And I do.

Clearing his voice, he continues, "If we come to an agreement, I'll expect you to go to work immediately."

"When I take a job, recreation is put aside."

He nods, leans on his elbows on the immaculately clean and clear desk, steeples his fingers and eyes me carefully. In a waiting room not unlike his I once picked up a magazine with an article on body language, and it said if you want to look wise and thoughtful, steeple your fingers and give a long stare. He does, but he doesn't.

He sighs deeply, then rises and walks to the window and stands staring out, hands folded thoughtfully behind his back. I remain silent, and he turns to face me. "I hate all this."

"It's a beautiful view," I offer, with a semi-shrug.

"All this. All this intrigue. I don't know why my daughter needs to get involved…"

"How so?"

"She was doing well at U.C. Berkeley, then the wheels fell off and her grades started going to hell and she stopped calling her mother or me."

"Drugs?" I ask.

"I hope not, but who knows. Over two months ago…almost three now…she disappeared and we've not heard from her…except via her trust."

"How so?" I ask again.

"Her trust. Her grandfather set up trusts for her, her brother, and her two cousins. And she's still drawing on hers. Drawing heavily the last two checks."

"Is it enough to interest a kidnapper?" I ask.

"Her portion is a little over seven million dollars, which she came into access to...at least some of it...less than six months ago when she turned twenty one."

"Some of it?"

"It seems a lot now, but when my father set it up almost sixty years ago, it wasn't so great a sum. He tied it to inflation and the draws to a percentage of the total, and the trust's investments have done rather well."

"You seem to be avoiding the question."

Again, he clears his throat before replying. "She can draw fifty thousand a month, and she's done so for the last three months and can continue doing so until it's zero."

He returns to his chair and flops down, this time looking more than just a little disgusted. I don't respond to the fifty grand a month, so he continues.

"It's got to stop. You've got to find her for me and put a stop to whatever she's doing."

I can't help but get a half smile and shake my head a little. "Mr. Remington, if your daughter is twenty one, there's not much you nor I can do, as she's an adult."

"But is she operating out of her own free will? I believe she's being held, and forced to draw out the funds...operating under duress. These eco-terrorists will stoop to anything."

"Then that's a different matter altogether."

He nods, now looking hopeful. "So, you think you can find her?"

"Obviously you've had the police searching for her?"

"She's been reported missing to the Berkeley police and to the FBI."

"And you're not satisfied with their efforts."

"What efforts? Here," he hands me a letter sized piece of stationery.

It reads: *Daddy, I'm fine. Don't bother trying to find me. I have a new life with people I admire, true environmentalists, and am helping to support their cause. You know I've long been active in PETA. Well, ARA is even more effective in the hunt for justice for those who can't obtain it for themselves. I'm happy. Love to you and Mamma. J.J.*

I drop it back on his desk. "Are you sure she wrote this?"

"Her fingerprints were on it."

"Anyone else's?"

"Two other sets. Which I can provide you."

"What's ARA?"

"Animal Revolutionary Army. It seems they're way more militant than PETA ever thought of being. I have a report of their activities...at least what they're suspected of."

"Her name, J. J.?"

"Her full name is Jane Jasper Remington...but she's called J. J."

"Why do you think the FBI is not doing their job?"

"They reported that an agent located her in Montana at some kind of encampment, and she identified herself then refused to talk with him, only telling him she was fine and to please leave her alone. I flew out there and couldn't get on the property. Armed guards and all that."

"So, what do you think I can do?"

"Bring her to me. All I want is a chance to talk with her, to make sure she's not drugged up, to get her out from under the influence of this ARA for a little while. Before she gets involved in something terrible."

Again, I have to smile. "You know if I take her against her will, it's kidnapping. She's an adult."

"I want to get her out of there and back to New York State. I have more than one friend who's a judge, and I can get an order to have her committed, but I have to get her back to New York."

"It's a seven million dollar trust. I get twenty percent for recoveries so I'll expect a million four if I get her back here. I'll need an advance of fifty thousand expenses against the fee."

I can see the businessman take over his demeanor, as his brows furrow. "That's a lot of money."

"Kidnapping is a capital crime. You're asking someone to take a lot of risk."

He's silent for a long time, staring out the window, then turns back to me. "You know we are against firearms and want this violence stopped...all over the country...it's a creeping cancer infecting the people of the United States...and the world for that matter."

"And I'm a proponent of guns and couldn't be more diametrically opposed to what you profess."

He furrows his brow but doesn't call security to have me escorted out. Then, his voice low and sincere, he asks, "Can you do this without firearms?"

"It's not that I can't, it's that I won't. It sounds like you are asking me to go into the lion's den, and I won't do so with a switch in hand. I have lots of scars from holing the short end of the stick."

"I'll have to think about it. It'll take my counsel a day or two to draw up an agreement."

Again, I laugh. "Mr. Remington, you don't want anything in writing regarding my employment. In fact, you'll probably want to destroy all evidence of this meeting."

He shakes his head in wonderment, then gets serious. "How do you know I'll pay you?"

"Do I look like a guy you'd want to stiff? Trust me, I do my job, you'll pay up."

That again causes him to stare out the window. Finally, he turns back. "I don't want anyone killed."

"If it comes to firearms, I'll try and not double tap the bad guys, if there are any bad guys involved."

He looks confused, so I add. "I'll only shoot them once. If I don't put the second one in their nasty evil skulls, there's always a chance they'll live."

"Oh, God," he says, and turns a little green.

I start to get up, but he stops me, "Wait."

So I slump back down.

"I had an agency pull a background on you after one of the oil companies I invest in referred you. There's not much in the file?"

His lip slightly curls on one side, an expression of contempt. But I'm not going to bite. "And I hope to keep it that way."

"It seems you've killed people before in your business?" He shakes his head.

"I was in Desert Storm, and yes, a few hajis got in the way of my AR, and my grenades, and yes, in pursuit of justice, I've had to kill some folks…but not since last week."

"Oh, God. How do you sleep at night?"

"Mr. Remington, read your Bible—"

"It says thou shalt not kill."

"Not in the original version, it says thou shalt not murder. And there's a lot of difference. But if you'll note, the Bible is full of killing. Do you think when God turned Lot's his wife into a pillar of salt, she wasn't dead? And one hundred other instances, including the state sanctioned murder of Christ. Sorry, but I could easily prosecute his killers, without benefit of judge and jury."

"Still, I don't think I could sleep. That was then, and this is today."

"And human nature is the same today as it was two thousand years ago, no matter what we'd like to believe…or I should probably say, as I believe you'd like to believe." I sigh deeply. "Mr. Remington, we all drag our own version of gargoyles around, monsters trailing us on a heavy chain, slathering at the mouth, growling, hating everything in their path...at least after you pass thirty and have some history. And yes, the little bastards nip at my butt from time to time. But I deal with it in my own way."

"Drugs?"

"Yes, if you consider Jack Daniels a drug. I have no interest in staying stupid for longer than it takes to sober up after a few hits on the bottle...besides, it's hard to look over your shoulder to see who's gaining on you if you're high on some rotten poison, booze included. I consider dope dealers the scum on the gene pool, so no, I don't do dope in the sense I think you mean. But I do do dope dealers when the opportunity presents itself."

"I don't know how you do that killing thing. By the way, are those Ostrich boots? Ostrich skin?"

I probably shouldn't, but I laugh. "Yeah, they are...but he died of old age."

"Bull hocky," he says, and looks at me like I'm Ostrich poop squeezing up between his toes, and I get the impression bull hocky's a major expletive for him.

He thinks I'm changing the subject. "So, where's the best steak in town?" Everyone likes being asked for their expertise.

"I like The Old Homestead over in the Meatpacking District."

I laugh again. "But you don't eat them unless they die of old age?"

He colors, and doesn't answer.

I rise. "I'm at the Waldorf. Give me a call if we have a deal. I'm going to take in the Met Museum and the

Planetarium this afternoon, and any other tourist thing I have time for, then I'll give the Old Homestead a try." I have to laugh aloud, not a smart thing to do when trying to make a deal with a hypocrite, but I can't help myself, then I add, "I may fly out tomorrow...the next day at the latest. I'll leave my cell number with the redhead."

"Oh, God," he says again, and mumbles, "I still don't know how you do it."

As I'm leaving I wave over my shoulder. "Nice meeting you, Mr. Remington. Good luck, whatever you decide. And, at first blush, I doubt that eco-terrorists have your daughter for eco's sake...it's something more than that. Odds are it's purely a money thing."

I close the door behind me, sensing him still sitting in stunned silence.

It's amazing to me how folks will compromise their values, or supposed values, when it's their ox being gored.

Chapter Three

He's right about one thing, the Old Homestead has one of the greatest steaks I've had the pleasure of caressing with my tongue. And I earned one after tromping through the Met for several hours.

My primary business is over, so it's playtime for a while longer.

The waiter clues me into Cielo, a club not far from where I'm chowing down. Funny thing is, when I wander up to the line to get in, I'm not that far from styling. More than one dude in line has on cowboy boots, but I think Justin or Tony Lama is not the designer of choice; these are far more flat-soled, far more metrosexual, but what the hell, I'll fit right in. I do give the door guy a look like a bull at a bastard calf when he hits me for a twenty-five buck cover charge. He's big, but gym rat big, and would go down in a heartbeat and cry for his mama if he thought he'd end up with a scar on his booze-puffy mug.

And the music, after I've done my twenty-minute penance in line, is anything but country, and so friggin' loud, bone shattering loud, it's hard to tell what genre it might be. It takes me another twenty minutes to get a drink, and that's another fifteen bucks for a watery Jack on the rocks…how you can water down a Jack rocks is a little beyond me, but if I have another, it'll be neat.

I finally see a lady who attracts me, a blond with straight hair to the shelf of a very nice gluteus maximus, and boobs that are palm-filling perfect that you would only have enough left to tease the nipple with your thumb, and the nipples show nicely as she's bra-less with only a little silk between the beauties and the cruel outside world. I sidle over next to her and her lady friend, and over the music, ask, "Hey, how about me buying you a drink and maybe you'll clue me in to what's happening in the neighborhood?"

Not my finest pick up line, but better than "what's your sign?"

She eyes me up and down, curls her lip in disdain, then smiles at her friend and says, "Tex here wants to buy us a drink."

"Fuck yes," her bud says.

"Preference?" I ask them both, although the one with the butch haircut I'd not planned to have on my guest list.

In moments I'm back with two sex-on-the-beach drinks, and am now down another forty bucks. But I have high hopes it's an investment.

I'm pretty eclectic when it comes to my taste in music, but the hammering coming from high mounted speakers, barely filtered through a thousand multicolored, obviously helium filled, balloons, each with a four foot or longer tether hanging down, all highlighted by multi-hewed blue lights, is about all my backcountry ears can stand. After I hand the ladies their drinks, I ask, "What do y'all call that music?"

Both of them laugh, then butch asks, "Y'all? Where you from, cowboy? Alabama?"

"Wyoming. And yeah, I've pushed some cattle in my day."

The prettier one smiles at me, but it's a condescending smile, and offers, "We call that techno...and it's hot. They spin some swaged-up indy rock and some rap in between. You a Tupac man?"

I can't help but shrug, as she might as well be speaking Swingalli, so I act as if I understand and really look around and check the crowd out. Freaks, about one in four, a few shirtless, all wearing lots of ink and spiked hair of various electric colors, and the others seem to be freak fans...and I'm suddenly wondering what the hell I'm doing here. I guess I'm widening my experience. Of course I've never hit myself in the head with a hammer to see what it feels like, which would also be widening my experience.

There's a dance floor full of folks, but what they're doing is a freak-fest as far as I'm concerned, with the jerky movements of automatons, which is not particularly attractive to me, and even less sexy. Suddenly I'm beginning to feel a little old, so I ask the pretty one, "Doesn't any place play The Boss or rock with a little more feeling to it?"

Both of them laugh and shake their heads. "You can't feel this stuff?" Butch asks. "Fuck, man, I feel it clean to the bottom of my well."

And I suddenly think her well is pretty wide and deep, and as pretty as the blond is wonder if I have any interest in falling in the well of either one of them. Just as I'm wondering, Butch, who's a couple of inches taller than the blond; grabs her by the back of the neck and begins to swab the back of her throat with a tongue like a camel's. Even as slow as I am, I begin to get that they're a couple.

I give them a sloppy salute and back off, hearing Butch cackle loudly as I leave, then yell after me, "Thanks for the fuckin' drink, schmuck."   I wave over my shoulder which is as much of a "you're welcome" as I can muster, then ask a passing waitress "Where's the boy's room?"

"We don't got one," she says, giving me a coy smile.

"No head?"

"It's unisex, Charley. What's your schticht...*Midnight Cowboy*?" I don't much value the question, so I don't answer with the *Unforgiven* or *Open Range* I'm thinking as she wouldn't understand, and wait for her to reply to my original one, and she does. "We got four of those, in the back, on either side."

I shoulder my way through the crowd, trying not to slop my Jack Daniels on anyone, not that most of them are dressed in a way that a slop would matter, and find a room with the symbol of both a man and woman on the door, and decide that I need to piss more than I need to worry about offending one of the freaks. As I enter, she's exiting, and I'm up against an Orphan Annie fuzzy redhead who's obviously wearing no bra under her tee shirt which says Supa Dupa Fly.

"Watch it, asshole," she says and thrusts her boobs out as if it's an invitation to do so, but I shine it and them and move on. I'm in a room with two door-less stalls, two urinals, and no lock on the door. I belly up to a urinal, begin to relieve myself, and glance over as the door opens and in comes a girl in a yellow leather outfit that must have cost her daddy a month's wages—even though there's not a lot of it—and she winks at me as she heads for a stall. She's got lots of flowing auburn hair right out of a Pantene shampoo ad, yellow mascara and brown lipstick, but, surprisingly, it all looks pretty damn sexy on her. The girl's got a set of pegs, nicely tanned, made even longer by five inch spike heels. The skirt barely covers the fuzz, if she has any. With the current styles as they are, I imagine she's shaved as close as most the chests of the male gender—if you can call them that—out on the dance floor. It's another quandary to me why a guy would shave, or wax, his arms and chest and then sport four days growth of beard.

I shake it off, both my wonder and my unit, tuck it in, zip up, and start for the door when I hear her yell, "Hey, big mon, you a real cowboy? You want a wild ride?"

"Got a date," I yell back, and am gone. It's not that I don't appreciate a beautiful, expensively dressed woman, but one wonders exactly what one's "getting into" in a freak show like this one, so I pass. Besides, in this crowd if you reach down there you never know what you might discover, and if I wrapped my hand around a set of fuzzy nuts I might just rip 'em off.

I slip through the crowd to the door, wave down a cab, and ask the Pakistani gentleman driving if he knows a nice quiet jazz club near the Waldorf. He shrugs and it dawns on me that I'm lucky he understood "Waldorf."

My iPhone vibrates in my pocket and I fish it out and see it's an unknown caller, and answer.

"We need to talk," the voice says, and I realize it's J. Cornelius Remington.

"Now?" I ask.

"I'm near the Waldorf. Bull and Bear in five minutes?"

"I'm probably twenty minutes away. I took your advice on the Old Homestead." I don't mention my incursion into the freak show.

"I'll be in the bar when you get there."

"You got it."

If I had to guess, I'd say I'm very close to being retained.

Chapter Four

J. Cornilius has changed out of his bib and tucker and has on an admirable camel hair sport coat, dark brown slacks, a soft shirt, croc belt and sockless loafers that probably cost a grand. He's at a small table against the window sipping what appears to be a Champagne cocktail, as there's a dissolving cube of sugar in the bottom of a flute filled with a golden liquid.

He doesn't bother with hello, but as soon as I sit, asks, "How about four hundred thousand?"

I give him a tightlipped smile and shake my head. "Look, pardner, I came a long ways to see if I can be of service and I came on my own dime. I enjoyed the museum and the planetarium, and a great steak in a classy hundred-year-old joint, so I'm fine with it. I wish you the best of luck finding your daughter and hope you do before she's carrying the whelp of some hippy druggie throwback and you end up with a mentally deficient drug dependent grandson." He reddens as I get up, nod, and turn to leave.

"Wait," he calls after me, so I pause and look back, and he continues, "please join me for a drink and we can talk this out."

I return just as a waiter comes tableside. I order a Jack up. Remington's quiet for a moment, so I ask, "I don't suppose you've ever been shot."

"With a gun, you mean?"

"I don't mean a flu shot." I have to laugh.

"Of course not."

"Well, I have, more than once, and to risk an understatement, it's no fun. And next time could likely be my last time. There's no negotiation on the price. It's standard for me. My last job was a two point five million dollar fee, so I'm no virgin when it comes to substantial fees...and I damn well earn them."

"Why are you convinced this will be so dangerous?"

"Do you recall..." My drink arrives so I hold for a second until the waiter gets out of earshot, "...do you recall telling me you were refused entrance to ARA's compound by armed guards?"

"Yes."

"Then my concern is reinforced by your own experience. I'll be happy to lend you a firearm if you'd like to go back and force your way into their inner sanctum."

He sighs and looks around the room as if searching for someplace to hide. I wait until his attention returns to me and the subject at hand, and finally he says, "One million four?"

"That's the magic number."

"But only upon your successful delivery of my daughter, in good health, to me here in New York state?"

"I only get paid if I perform."

"Other than the expense advance, which is against the fee. So I'll owe a million three fifty? Will you return the fifty thousand if you're unsuccessful?"

"No, I won't." I'm getting a little irritated. "You're a regular math whiz."

"No reason to be sarcastic."

"Do we have a deal?"

Again, a deep sigh, but he answers in the affirmative with a nod of the baldhead.

"I'll expect you to have a complete file for me. All personal data, all account numbers, all credit card info, all past addresses, and the address of this ARA compound, and everything, and I mean *everything,* you can supply on your daughter. And I'd like it before noon tomorrow as I have a five PM flight."

He looks more than a little disturbed. "All financial information, her account numbers? How do I know—"

"Mr. Remington, we have an understanding and an agreement totally based on trust. If you can't trust me with everything, and I mean everything, then we should part, wishing each other well—"

"Sorry, sorry. I'm just not used to doing business this way."

"This, sir, is an unusual circumstance and may require unusual methods to accomplish, which is why you contacted me in the first instance. My methods are all out of the box. So, is it yes or no?"

This time he doesn't hesitate. "Drop by the office at ten and I'll have it for you, along with a check for fifty thousand."

"Cash, no check. Messenger it over. I'm going to sleep in. I'll have a cell phone delivered to your office, which I'd appreciate your keeping at hand at all times as it will be our primary means of communication. My number will be programed into it…but please don't call me unless you have pertinent information to convey. Wish me luck," I say, down my drink, and rise to leave.

I'm a little surprised to see him tear up and backhand a tear from his eye. But he stands and extends a hand, clears his throat, and with a more than merely sincere tone asks, "Please, find my daughter and bring her safely home."

"If I can't, no one can." I wave over my shoulder, and head for my room.

Chapter Five

I've only had some slight experience with those being called eco-terrorists.

While doing a bodyguard job, watching after a young country singer who was beginning to hit it big—Tammy Houston—I snatched the wrist of a hippy girl who'd just thrown paint on Tammy's fur coat. The hell of it was the coat was faux fur, and not that expensive. That didn't keep me from turning the young lady over my knee, right outside the Gaucho restaurant on 2nd Street in downtown Seattle, and tanning her butt until she bawled like a baby.

Tammy fired me on the spot and I spent the night in the hoosegow...not for the spanking, but for breaking the jaw of one long-hair and the arm of another who decided to come to the property destroying hippy girl's rescue. I take umbrage when someone is stupid enough to pull a two-inch blade penknife on me, and I broke his arm to cure him of stupidity, and the jaw of the other as he called me a son-of-a-bitch and a cocksucker. Son-of-a-bitch I don't mind so much, as I'm sure they are not really casting aspersions on my mom.

It doesn't pay to beat up on rich-kid-liberals in Seattle. No good deed goes unpunished. I paid a five thousand dollar fine and did four weeks of community service in a Seattle soup kitchen serving goulash to guys who drove up in BMW's. Truthfully, not all of them drove up in anything, as many actually needed a hot meal. Having never begged, I'm not positive, but suspect it's much easier to work for a living.

I even made a few new friends while on the job, including a priest, Father Sean O'Donnel, who runs the joint. I traded some carpentry work—hanging doors—for a basement room while I paid my penance. I could have afforded a nearby hotel room, but one adds to life's experiences as one can…and I did.

As it turned out the judge did me a favor with the community service as I recognized a guy for whom I was dishing up some slop; a guy who'd skipped a hundred grand bail in Las Vegas. I called the bondsman, got a contract, put the guy facedown on the sidewalk after his next bummed bowl of soup and collected a twenty grand recovery fee for hauling him into the same lockup I'd recently left.

God works in mysterious ways.

And, come to think of it, Tammy still owes me for that week's work. I'm not holding my breath.

The long-hairs' medical bills cost me fourteen thousand, so, after my three grand premium to a local bondsman, a few expenses, and the medical bills, I came out a grand ahead.

Pax has emailed me another report on ARA, this time with background info on its leaders.

Arnold Rostov seems to be the man in charge, and he's no slouch when it comes to paramilitary background, having come out of a short tour with the Army Rangers, followed by a short visit to their graystone hotel at Fort Levenworth…four years for assaulting an officer. He also did a tour with Blackwater in Iraq. He's been clean since, almost ten years, but his subordinates are even more colorful. I've gotta believe that his worry about the world's animals is a total scam, as it seems he's dispatched his share, particularly the two legged variety.

His two lieutenants are both ex-cons. Terrel Hutchins did a nickel in Huntsville for bankrobbery; Margaret McFadden, an older broad who once ran with the Black Panthers, did two years in California's Chowchilla Women's Prison for possession after pleading down from intent-to-sell.

Most of the underlings have done county time for destruction of property, possession, vandalism, and concealed carry...but none over a year. And most of them for ARA related activity.

John Sainz—nickname "Saint"—is probably there for what he thinks is a moral reason, as he flunked out of veterinary school in Davis, California. Pauly Rook, likewise morally affronted by perceived cruelty to animals, was Boston born, Harvard educated, and a doper. Norvin Zimmerman, nickname "Sixpack," is most likely there for the money as he's a ex-Navy shore patrolman, discharged for abusing a female prisoner. Likewise, a tall, skinny guy who looks almost albino, Craig Pasternak, nickname "Pasty" is only muscle; and Charley Many Dogs, nickname "Mutt" who's an ex-cop from Billings, Montana and was fired for taking kickbacks from prostitutes. The latter three are reputed to be armed guards for the group, but all of them have been known to carry at one time or another.

An interesting bunch, and there are another forty or so members at a Maxville, Montana compound who have, so far, gone unnamed.

I almost wish I'd flown directly to Montana, but there are a few things I need from my ministorage in Vegas, and since the ARA seems a hippy culture, I might as well drive my van up to the Big Sky country. If I painted it with flowers I'd be sure to fit right in.

A couple of jobs ago, I had to head for Williston, North Dakota and the Bakken oilfields. As Williston has the most expensive entry apartment cost in the country, due to the oil boom, I said to hell with it and invested in a Ford 250 and a camper, which to me is the lap of luxury...but my Dodge van is pretty comfortable with a cot, a Porta-Potty and, far more important to my profession, hideout compartments for a variety of weaponry. It also has magnetic stripes and various magnetic signs so I can change my calling whenever. I can be a plumber, a pizza delivery truck, or even a SWAT van with the addition of a few signs and a few lights. I also have a number of license plates hidden therein. And she's powered with a polished and relieved Hemi and can dust most pursuit vehicles, particularly since I keep a bag full of tetrapods under the front seat which will blow the tires of most anything following other than a Humvee battleground equipped.

I also have replaced my Harley Sportster, destroyed not long ago, with an Iron 883 model which I had a buddy trick out with black paint, flames, and even more chrome. I'm tempted to drive it to beautiful Montana as it's early summer, and a beautiful trip, but I can't take all I fear I'll need on the bike. Weapons I'll need as some of these boys may be packing heavy. I could add bags to the bike, but she's so pretty I hate to screw up her lines. Even then long-arms couldn't make the trip.

My buddy Pax is waiting for me at the curb at 7:30 p.m., as agreed, and has reservations at my favorite Vegas Italian joint, Piero's, where we will consume some animals—much, I'm sure, to the chagrin of those I plan to visit after a long drive up Highway 15 to Montana.

Chapter Six

Pax Weatherwax is my closest friend, my sometimes partner, my most trusted adviser, and the provider of most of what makes me look smart to the rest of the world—which is no easy task. My buddy Paxton Weatherwax was a fellow Desert Storm Marine who kept my ugly mug from pushing up daisies, and did so numerous times. I did repay the favor at least once. The last time he kept me from going cold, he lost an inch and a half out of his left thigh thanks to an AK47. Still, even with a platform shoe, I'd take him as a back-up before ninety-nine-point-nine percent of the supposedly tough guys I've come across. For all his attributes as a tough S.O.B., he's even smarter than he is tough. He's turned his disability pay into a business as an Internet service provider with offices in four cities. He's kept me invisible to those who'd like to do me harm, including the U.S. Government, routed my dough and messages through a half dozen cities in as many countries, and dug up information needed in my dubious endeavors and the subjects of my attentions. Information to rival the NSA.

Pax is able to put a Trojan Horse program into almost any computer if he can discover their IP address, and thus trace the computer's activities, including every key stroke. He uses programs like Spokeo.com to dig up info and those of interest, finds pictures posted on social sites and uses their EXIF tags to get GPS locations of where they were taken, tracks cell phones to determine their location, and even taps into several "life style" companies to snatch their info. He also uses a couple of guys in India and Malta who receive my email, and that of other Weatherwax Internet Services clients, and buries it so deeply I presume even the NSA has trouble tracking and deciphering it. He's a very smart dude.

And he's more than just a buddy. I'd get between him and a hungry lion, should it come to that.

As I climb in his CJ7, he throws a folder in my lap. He drives, and I read and view aerials of the ARA compound just west of a little Montana burg called Maxville. The town is split by a scenic drive, Highway 1, with half on one side in the Flint Range and half on the other in the John Long Mountains—the road being a dividing line. The camp is up a fairly narrow lodgepole pine covered ravine in the John Longs, about three miles from the village, backing up to a section owned by a mining company. Beyond that is some very wild country and a million acres of national forest. There are six buildings total, the use of which Pax has been unable to identify as Google Earth displays no building elevations in these remote areas. I find it interesting, and a little suspicious, that a group involved in illegal activities would have only one entrance and exit road.

Of even more interest is additional background material he's unearthed, much of which is on eco-terrorism in general, and more on the Hutchins, McFadden and Sainz in particular.

I quickly learn that prior to 9/11 the FBI considered eco-terrorism the country's greatest threat. A group called the Animal Liberation Front was the primary culprit, followed closely by Earth Liberation. The two groups were estimated by the FBI to have committed more than 1,100 crimes, causing more than one hundred million bucks in damage. Michigan State University's mink research farm alone lost millions due to the actions of the groups.

I like animals. I haven't had a dog since before I went into the Marine Corps, when I didn't replace a chocolate lab I'd had since before high school. I'll have another dog someday, if I live long enough, and I'll treat it as if it were part of the family because I think a dog, or a horse, becomes just that.

Still, I understand the food chain, and will never put an animal above a human if it comes to making a choice. It's a matter of who's on top, animal or man. Not that I wouldn't have sacrificed some worthless humans if I had to choose between them and Buster, my old lab. But I consider those a-holes sub-human.

Among the many crimes committed, or suspected to have been committed by ARA, are raids on mink farms, on bobcat and lynx farms, and on drug facilities where animals are used for experimentation. The latter is a sick business, but would you trade a sister or brother, son or daughter, whose life depended upon a new drug, for the life of a monkey?

Now if they were testing cosmetics or some such nonsensical substance, and killing animals, I might be sympathetic. But not if the testing were to formulate a drug that might save a million human lives.

Life is full of choices, and sometimes you have to choose your own species over another.

ARA, it seems, carries their destructive activities a step farther than other groups. It not only releases animals, but releases the valuables from vaults and safes of the places they raid. One wonders what the real motivation of the group might be. More than one ARA member has been convicted of possession with intent to sell, and I have to wonder if a little cannabis, or even some methamphetamine is not part of the scheme of things around ARA'ville?

I haven't had a mountain outing for a long time, so I'm looking forward to a stroll in the woods, where a guy can carry a long arm and look just like a hundred other guys who stroll the woods.

After supper I visit my ministorage on Tropicana in Vegas. Seeing my Harley there changes my mind and I load her up in the back of the van. Who knows...mountain country, great weather, and she might be able to go where the van can't.

It's a little over nine hundred miles from Vegas to Maxville and, loafing along, I make it to Pocatello, Idaho on the first leg. It's an easy run to western Montana on the second leg and I get to the very small community of Maxville in time for lunch at the Veterans of Foreign Wars hall—the only bar in town—if you can call it a town, as it's really a lot of homes on acreage, spread out up a couple of canyons, with the only bar just off the highway. The joint is a great country bar, with a pool table, three poker and keno machines, and an elk head and two deer heads gracing the wall. By the four pickup trucks and one old Subaru lined up outside you can pretty well determine the clientele. There's only a half-dozen guys in the place, and a lady behind the bar.

I push through the door and only get a glance or two from the patrons. Taking a stool, one of only seven at the bar, at the far end away from the door I order a long neck Moose Drool beer. Four guys who look like construction types—then, I decide, loggers due to their plaid shirts, suspenders, and Carthartt knit caps and multi-pocketed pants—are at a table playing cribbage. Two older guys who look like ranchers—cowboy hats, wrangler jeans, and scuffed boots with riding heels a dead giveaway—are at the far end of the bar nearest the door, with four stools separating me from them.

None of them look like hippy eco-terrorists, in fact all of them look like they'd be more than happy to feed eco-terrorists or hippies to the grizzly bears who frequent the mountains. Maxville's about halfway between Glacier National Park and Yellowstone National Park, so there's no telling what critters wander the surrounding mountains.

They all, and the barmaid, seem happy enough to let me sip my beer in peace. She's a sight, with purple pedal pushers and a pink blouse, hair a little like she used a kitchen mixer on it rather than a comb, and one front tooth gone black. But she's nice enough, and gives me an extra toothy grin when I push a seventy-five cent tip into the trough behind the bar.

Just as I'm about to finish and head out to find a campground to hole up for the afternoon and finish reading Pax's voluminous background material, the front door swings aside. The bright light floods the room and I have to shade my eyes and squint, but soon see it's three bearded guys, one of them big enough to eat hay and crap in the road. The other two look fit enough—in fact I'd guess gym rats by the slope of their shoulders and the fact

43

that knotted necks begin flaring out from the bottom of their ears.

The dynamics of a small public place are interesting. You can suddenly feel the added weight of the air in the joint at the same time it goes silent. The attitude of everyone formerly laughing has gone sour, even without comments.

The new guys trade glares with the four at the table as they cross the room, then take the three stools nearest me.

As they belly up to the bar, the two older cowboys down their drinks, and I hear one of them say, "Fuck this, it's starting to smell in here." He meets the stare of the three hairy-faced lads, and they don't back down a bit, but rather stare the cowboys all the way out of the place. Only then do they turn to the barmaid and order. And I come to the conclusion I've ordered hippy fare, as all of them order Moose Drool.

I can see that the barmaid, a pleasant enough girl with tiny boobs under the pink blouse, but wide hips under the purple pedal pushers—a little pear shaped—is doing her best to be congenial, and asks the three new guys, "How's things with the critter folks?"

The one in the middle, who I'm beginning to guess is the Harvard boy I've read about in Pax's report, as he's so blond as to almost be white headed, answers, "Things are fine. You didn't see the Schwan's truck around today?"

"Nope," she answers with a smile. "Maybe he broke down. The store up in Phillipsburg is open till nine, if y'all need something, or back down in Drummond...I think they close at seven."

"We can wait till tomorrow," he says, then ignores her, and she starts down the bar my way, wiping it as she comes.

The biggest of the three, trunk about the size of a fifty-gallon drum, is on the stool closest to me. He glances over and eyes me up and down, then growls through his scraggly beard and mustache which is too thin to make much of an impression, "What the fuck are you eyeballing, white-eye?" and only then do I realize he's Indian.

I shrug and smile my most winsome grin. "Just taking in the sights. And my eyes aren't white, at least not the last time I looked." I'm grinning foolishly and it makes him a little bemused.

"You're big enough, but you ain't no threat, dickwad," he says, and turns back to his buddies.

The barmaid stops from her trip toward the backroom and steps back across from the Indian, and her tone is no longer pleasant. "Charley, you still haven't paid all you owe for busting up the furniture last time...so don't you be starting any trouble. This guy was just setting here minding his own busin—"

"And why don't you mind yours, pussy face?" he growls at her, and she turns red in the face, spins on her heel, and continues heading for the back room.

I'm eyeballing his profile, wondering if the long neck is heavy enough to smash his broad nose even flatter, but don't have time to do so, as I see in the mirror behind the bar, a chair coming down hard.

Looks like it's lumberjacks against the ARA.

Not that it's any surprise to me.

Chapter Seven

I leap to the side away from the Indian as the chair smashes across his head, splintering the leg struts.

"Goddamn," the guy in the middle of the three says, and jumps to the far side.

The Indian just shakes his head as if he's been slapped, then spins on the stool to face the lumberjack who's wrecked a bar chair. Another of the lumberjack types is right behind the first, and puts a decent right into the chops of the middle guy, and the third jumps up and squares away before another of the table guys gets to him, and they begin wailing away.

I'm a little amused by the whole thing, and step back toward the end of the bar and the doorway into the back room, where the barmaid has disappeared, just as she shows up.

The proverbial ka ka has hit the fan. It's assholes and elbows, beer bottles and blood, as the two gym rats and the horse-big Indian swing haymakers and roundhouse punches, trading blows and knees and kicks with the lumberjacks. They're smacking each other pretty good but doing little damage other than drawing blood and tiring themselves out…but there's plenty of all of that.

I can't help but chuckle, and the barmaid looks over and snaps, over the noise of blows and crashing furniture. "You think this is funny?"

"Pretty damn funny," I reply.

"If you was gettin' your ass kicked you wouldn't think so. That's my boyfriend that Charley has on the floor, about to kill."

"Buy me a beer and I'll save his ass?" I offer.

"Charley will kill you," she says.

"Bet me a beer?" I say, and give her a silly grin.

"Whatever,...the sheriff is on his way."

Charley, the Indian, is astride one of the lumberjacks, pounding the dog doo out of him as the guy is trying to cover his face with his forearms, so I step over and plant one of my hiking boots about six inches deep in the Indian's ribs. He oofs and rolls off the guy to the far side, grabbing his side as if he might have a broken rib—or four, I hope.

One of the other ARA gym rats, the albino, has a lumberjack under each arm—a double headlock—while the other is trading blows with the fourth guy, and they bang their way through the front door and are outside.

As the Indian is trying to decide if he's hurt, the albino is facing me, a lumberjack's head under each arm. So each arm is tied up. I can't help but grin at him at his foolishness as I step forward and bring a hard kick up into his crotch.

He turns green as he releases the two guys and windmills his arms as he falls back across the pool table, then pukes all over the green felt. It'll be a while before it's fit for a game of eight ball.

No good deed goes unpunished. The two guys he's been throttling are up and, seeing me but not recognizing me for the savior I am, both charge forward. I guess I looked like one of the opposition as I was drinking a Moose Drool. Should have ordered my usual Jack neat.

I drop to the side, plant a hand on the floor, and kick the leading one a sidekick to the knee. He folds like a cheap towel in front of the other one, who stumbles across him as I get to my feet, and is going down to both hands stiff armed on the floor as I bring a knee up.

Both of them are suddenly out of the fight, one rolling on the floor, his knee up in his chest in both hands as he screams like a mating eagle; the other is rolling on the floor next to him, both hands covering his nose trying to control the blood gushing between his fingers.

But it's not over, as the Indian is back on his feet, and reaches for a bar stool to crease my skull. I step in and I hit the big man a driving right into his Adam's apple, and his eyes bulge as he stumbles backwards, then collapses with his big butt on the bar foot-railing and his back to the bar. His eyes are bulging the size of golf balls. He's trying like hell to catch his breath, wheezing like a horse who's just run the Derby, and I'm hoping I haven't smashed his larynx and killed the dumb fuck.

A manslaughter trial and five to fifteen years in Montana's Deer Lodge Prison would upset my "rescue Jane Jasper Remington" schedule.

It seems the trouble is over, but maybe it's just begun, as a county-mountie busts through the door, sap in one hand, Glock in the other.

And the way he's waving the Glock around, he's young and maybe a little too eager to shoot somebody!

Chapter Eight

"All of you," the cop shouts, "against the wall, face it, hands over your head." He's cutting his eyes around so rapidly I fear he'll get dizzy and go to his knees.

I comply quickly, not wanting to upset a young guy who has probably never fired his weapon other than on the range.

The big Indian is still on the floor, but seems to be catching his breath, as the rest of us face the wall.

"He may be hurt!" the barmaid, who hasn't moved from behind the bar, exclaims.

The young cop, foolish as only the young can be, moves over and extends his hand to help the Indian to his feet, his gun in his other hand, now down at his side.

I guess the big guy has no interest in going to the pokey, and as he takes the kid's hand, he jerks him hard and the cop's head crashes into the edge of the hardwood bar. His eyes roll up in his head and his firearm skitters across the barroom floor. He folds without a twitch and doesn't move.

The big boy is trying to get to his feet and rolls to his hands and knees. In four steps I'm there and drive another hiking boot deep into his ribs on the other side from the first kick, and he rolls over the cop. He's not finished, and is still trying to get to his feet. He's a very tough Indian.

However, probably not as tough as the pool cue that's on the floor near my feet, so I gather it up and put it to good use. I learned long ago that you have to be very careful hitting a guy in the head with anything harder than your fist, so I make it a glancing blow. It's enough, and finally he plants his face in the floor. As quickly as I've picked it up, I wipe my prints off and deposit it back on the floor.

I snatch up the cop's Glock and wave the others back against the wall, then turn to the bar maid. "Bring me a glass of water."

The cop is still not moving, so I sprinkle a little water on his face. It's pretty obvious that he's taken a good whack, as there's a growing goose-egg at the hairline over his right eye. I'm hearing a siren approaching from outside, so it's time to look like a white knight. Besides, I'm a little worried about the kid.

He begins to sputter, so I take a chance, again wipe my prints with my shirttail and shove his pistol back in his holster, then drag him over where his back can lean against the bar front. He's still not focusing as I hear a vehicle slide to a stop outside as its siren winds down.

I climb back on a bar stool, give the barmaid a wink, and suggest "You owe me a beer."

She nods, but replies "Later, big boy. But thanks, I think my boyfriend is gonna live...after a few stitches. You did kick him pretty hard. Hope you didn't break his leg."

"Sorry about that, but he came after me. Fact is, a couple of scars give a guy character," I say, just as the door slams aside and an older uniform, under a hundred x beaver cowboy hat, stomps in. His gun is still holstered. He's not a particularly big guy, but well put together and in good shape for a guy with as much gray as he has showing under his Stetson. His look is all business and it's obvious this is hardly his first rodeo.

"Is he hurt?" he asks, motioning with a nod of his head at the kid still on the floor.

"I'm...I'm okay," the young cop manages, trying to get to his feet.

"And that one," he says, giving a head feint at the Indian. "Looks like one of my frequent guests," he says, and gives the barmaid a wink. Then gets serious again.

The older guy walks over and puts a hand on the kid's shoulder. "Stay down, Johnny. I got this."

"I'm okay, Sheriff," he says.

"Stay down, hoss," the bossman says, and his voice rings with authority. "Now," he commands, "none of y'all move an inch...what the hell is going on here?"

The barmaid starts a long explanation, and I'm happy to say, closes with "none of this was the stranger's fault." I guess...I hope...I'm the only stranger.

As she finishes, another vehicle slides up outside and in walks a Montana Highway Patrolman. He's a tall guy with dirty blond hair, ice blue eyes, and a razor sharp nose. He too looks as if he's been around the barn a time or two.

"Hi, Matt," the sheriff addresses him and gets a "howdy" in return. Then the sheriff asks, "How about you taking the Carhartt bunch outside and interview them. I don't know if there's gonna be any charges yet, but go ahead and read them their rights if you would."

"Who put that knot on Johnny's head?" the MHP guy asks, and looks as if he's ready to return the favor.

"I'm about to find that out," the Sheriff replies.

After a half-hour, I'm surprised when all the old boys, even the Indian, are sent on their way after each of them plops a hundred bucks on the bar. It's taken ten minutes for the Indian to come to, but he does, and I guess since he was considered a victim, he, too, is cut loose. But not until he gives me a very hard look and simulates a gun with his hand, firing about six shots into my chest. I merely laugh and shake my head. He remains humorless.

I'm really surprised he walks, as he rapped the deputy pretty hard. Only in Montana.

Again to my surprise, the sheriff sends the deputy with the MHP guy, asking if he'll drop him off at the Medical center in Phillipsburg for a checkup, then joins me at the bar and orders a beer.

"You get no heat for drinking on the job?" I ask.

"What are you, Internal Affairs? Oh, I forgot," he laughs, "we ain't got no Internal Affairs department." He winks at the barmaid, then turns his attention back to me. "I'll be off duty in thirty minutes and I started two hours early this morning. When you only got four deputies you're on duty all the damn time." He eyes me up and down. "You can carry concealed in most of Montana, including here in Granite County...still, don't think I haven't noticed that lump in the small of your back."

"Not hiding it," I say. "It's permitted."

"Good thing you didn't pull it during this donnybrook," he says.

"No need," I say.

"Okay, good answer." He looks me up and down with an appraising look, then asks, "Now, sunshine, where you from and what's your story? I need a reason not to assist you in visiting our little cold rock hoosegow."

Chapter Nine

I smile, and shrug. "How about the fact I didn't do anything to warrant a visit?"

"I guess since I'm the sheriff I'll be the judge of that. This ain't the big city, son. I can throw you in just cause I don't like the way you look." He gives me a quick nod, assuring me he's more than willing to do just what he says.

"No question, Sheriff. It's your county."

"So, again, who are you and where you from?"

I make a quick decision to tell him at least most of the truth. "I'm Mike Reardon, originally from Sheridan. We're neighbors, sort of."

"You said 'originally'?"

"I did. I did a couple of tours in the Marine Corps and have been kicking around since, doing some bail enforcement—"

"Bounty hunter," he says, and nods knowingly.

"And some bodyguard work, and lots of recovery...not only skips, but property."

"Interesting," he says, and I get the nod again.

"It pays the bills," I say.

"So, how long you been here and how long you plan on staying?"

"Just rolled in. This was my first stop. I saw the sign 'scenic highway' and thought I'd take in the scenery and fish for a few days. I'll be staying in my van."

"So, why good ol' Maxville, Montana?"

"Just seeing the sights. It's beautiful—"

"Bullshit, sunshine. You're working and I'd like to know at what."

"Going to work a fly rod and beat the water with a number five line and a wooly bugger or coachman, if you can direct me to where to get a three day license."

"Again, bullshit. But if that's the way you want to play it. You up for a little advice?"

"Yes, sir."

"Your bail enforcement officer's badge, if you even got one, won't keep you from testing our jail menu. If you've got work in my county, I want to know what and whom, or I might get real crotchety. Understand?"

"Yes, sir. Where's the best fishing?"

"Al here can tell you better than I can."

"Al?"

The barmaid walks over—she's been listening as she polishes glasses—and extends a hand. I shake and ask, "Al?"

"I'm from Alabama...it kinda got shortened down over the years."

"Al it is," I say, and laugh. "You're the best lookin' Al I've ever seen." It's a bit of an exaggeration, but a little flattery never hurts.

She repeats what she told the sheriff when he first walked in. "This here fella didn't start any of that ruckus, sheriff. He only stepped in when I asked him to help out. And he sure as hell-is-hot stopped some of it. It coulda been lots worse."

The sheriff upends his beer, draining the long neck, and stands. He extends a hand. He's not a big guy, but he's got a handshake like one and calluses thick as horseshoes on his hands.

He tips his hat, "Welcome to Granite County. Keep your nose clean."

"Yes, sir. You sure I can't buy you a beer?"

"Mama gets upset I have more than one."

Al gives him a wave as he heads for the door. "Give Martha a big howdy for me."

He waves over his shoulder and is gone.

I drink the rest of the beer Al has bought me, and over the course of two more—which I pay for—get filled in on all the old boys who were involved in the disagreement. Like most local bartenders, she knows most everything about everyone.

Her boyfriend is a logger—a sawyer she tells me—and unfortunately one of the guys who came after me and who took a fairly hard side-kick to the knee. He'll be limping a while. Just as I'm draining the last of my third beer and getting ready to check out a couple of two-track forest service roads that Al has clued me into—roads that flank the canyon containing the ARA encampment—he gimps back into the bar. He doesn't look happy, but he doesn't look like he wants to go another round. So I turn back facing the bar, rest my forearms there, and order another.

He drags a leg and climbs up on the bar four stools down from me, turns my way and glowers for a moment as Al pours him a draft and as she says, "The sheriff said for you guys to stay out of here for the rest of the day."

"He's headed back to Phillipsburg. Hey," he snaps at me, "you fucked my knee up real good. I won't be able to work."

I spin, facing him. "You came at me, old buddy. I just gave you a love tap."

"No fucking work, for a week. God damn it."

"So, you know the country around here?"

"Ever tree and boulder and pile of bear shit."

"So, how much do you make knocking down trees, or whatever it is you do?"

"About twenty bucks an hour, not that it's any of your—"

"That's fine. I'll pay you the same for guiding me. A week's work guaranteed."

That stops him short and he stares at me. And finally manages, "It ain't hunting season."

"I know that. I want a guide to show me around is all. And you know every rock, or so you say."

Al jumps in, seeming eager for him to make a buck. "He does, he growed up here and knows his way 'round better than anybody."

"What's your name?" I ask, and extend a hand as I slip down the bar to take a seat next to him.

He looks hesitant for a moment, then takes the hand and shakes. He's no wuss and I'm glad I sank the handshake deep.

"Hunter Manovitch."

"You want the job or not?"

"How do I know you're good for it?"

"You're a trusting soul." I shake my head, then add, "How about I pay you cash money at the end of every day?"

"Suits me. When do we start?"

"Soon as we finish our beers."

"Where do we start?" he asks.

"Let's grab a table." Al looks a little hurt that she won't be in the conversation, but we head to a table as far as we can get out of earshot.

As soon as we're seated, I admonish him, "My business is private and you can't talk about it, not even to Al, understand?"

He shrugs. "Sure."

"I'm serious as a heart attack, Manovitch. I'll take it real personal you mouth around what we do."

This time his look is questioning. "So, is this legal stuff?"

"I don't break the law," I assure him with a lie. I don't mention that if I do break the law, I'll keep him out of it.

"Okay, I don't tell anyone what we're up to. You looking for gold or sapphires or something?"

"Nope, I'm looking for a lady."

Chapter Ten

Montana's Highway 1 is a scenic two lane alternate route making a big loop, maybe one hundred miles, from Anaconda near east-west Interstate 90, past Georgetown Lake and it's nearby ski mountain, Discovery, then through an old mining—now ranching and tourist—town of Phillipsburg, and again joining up with I-90 at Drummond. Anaconda is the home of a huge copper mine and Drummond bills itself as the "Bull Shipping" capital of the world, and means it literally.

Maxville and Hall are wide spots in the road along the loop.

Phillipsburg, also on the loop, is the county seat of Granite County—a county with a total population of just over four thousand. The John Long Range, where the ARA encampment is located, the Flint Range, and the magnificent Anaconda Pintler Range of mountains surround the scenic highway and little towns, rising from valley bottoms to alpine hard shouldered, normally snow covered, ridges.

The country is rolling grazing land and pine and fir covered mountains, populated with an independent strain of folks, most of whom make their living with their hands, horses, chainsaws, and an abundance of guts.

Needless to say, it's sparsely populated.

The Anaconda Pintler Wilderness makes up the southern part of the county and is topped by the Continental Divide in the Anaconda Pintler Mountains. Its cloud covered high and rugged rock peaks are full of cirques, U-shaped valleys, and glacial moraines. Most of the year pristine lakes and tumbling streams are fed by water running off the snowfields above the timberline. Lakes and streams are where the hardy find fishing for several species of native and introduced trout and char. On the southwest side of the divide your canoe will take you, eventually, to Seattle; on the northeast, eventually, to New Orleans, if you can get around the man-made obstructions.

Black bears and an occasional grizzly—the area is halfway between Glacier and Yellowstone National Park—moose, elk, mule deer, mountain goat, big horn sheep, cougar, wolf, and wolverine make their home here.

Elevations range from 5,100 feet lush valley bottoms to the 10,793 foot West Goat Peak. Sagebrush and willow flats and some of Montana's finest graze are found in the lower elevations where the west fork of Rock Creek, Flint Creek, and The Clark Fork meander. Slopes gradually rise to forests of pine, fir, and spruce, then more steeply to aspen, whitebark pine, and sub-alpine larch. The highest and most imposing slopes are often bare except for lichen covered talus. Forty-five miles of the three thousand plus mile Continental Divide National Scenic Trail traverses the length of the wilderness.

It's the spine of this great country.

Since the white man sent trappers and hunters into the country where once only Blackfeet, Shoshoni, and Salish Indians tread—and maybe even before—the wild country harbored those who didn't want to be found or their business known, and still does.

It's the high lonely at its best—and its worst. And it's country I love and am familiar with, having been raised in the similar mountains of North Wyoming.

The ARA compound occupies a narrow canyon floor crisscrossed by a three-foot wide stream, shaded by narrow-leaf cottonwoods, flanked by thick forests of lodgepole pine—so thick they are difficult to traverse, particularly as the slope rises higher and higher. The camp access road leads west off of Highway 1 and dead ends at their gate. However, higher on the mountain sides above it run a pair of Deer Lodge Forest Service two-track roads that lead deeper into the national forest—the ARA property is a one hundred sixty acre half-mile square island surrounded by public land.

Both Al and Hunter have estimated that as many as three dozen of the ARA faithful occupy the compound, from kids in their late teens to a woman, with gray hair to her waist whom the locals refer to, jokingly, as Mother Superior.

Margaret 'Maggie' McFadden is in her sixties and, along with a guy named Terrel Hutchens—nickname Terry—seem to be Arnold Rostov's lieutenants. Maggie is hardly my idea of 'mother superior.' As Pax has reported, back when she was a whelp she ran with the Black Panthers and likes her men big, black, and profane. She did two years for possession, Chowchilla Women's Prison, pleading down from intent to sell. She's adorned with lots of ink, most one color prison tats, including devils and skulls. Mother superior she ain't.

Terrel "Terry" Hutchins is also an ex-con. A trained mountain climber who once scaled a four storey building in order to gain entrance to a State Savings and Loan. Hutchins did a nickel in Huntsville. Brooding, heavy browed, barrel chested, now with a slight pot belly but ox strong, he too is covered with lots of ink. The rumor is he's in charge of the muscle at ARA.

Both Maggie and Terry, and many other ARA members, occasionally show up at the little Maxville saloon. Rostov never does. Some of this I've gleaned from Pax's background material, some from Al and Hunter.

Catching up with my reading I determine who the three ARA boys in the bar were: Norvin 'Sixpack' Zimmerman did a five year tour as a Shore Patrolman in the Navy, stationed stateside. He was discharged after being suspected of abusing a prisoner, believed to be an armed guard for ARA; Craig Pasternak, Pasty, almost white hair, sunburns easily, gangly tall but a decent athlete, a highly rated soccer player, now an armed guard for ARA; and last but certainly not least, Charley Many Dogs, Mutt to his buddies, big bellied Crow Indian, ex-cop from Billings and before that the Crow Reservation, who did a year for taking prostitution kickbacks, easily recognized with a jagged scar across his forehead from going through a windshield.

Pax has given me info on eight of the players in ARA, but it seems there're another twenty seven or so I know little about...but he said he'll keep digging, and if I know Pax he'll soon have a Trojan Horse planted in one or all of ARA's computers, and we'll know every email they send and every key stroke.

It seems I'm ready to go to work.

Chapter Eleven

Hunter has a Jeep, an older CJ7, so I make a deal with him to throw it into the mix for another fifty bucks a day, with me buying the fuel. He's thrilled and I don't have to break out my Harley to ride the back-country dirt, rock strewn roads. He also has a cabin a mile or so up the Maxville road which heads east into the Flint Range, and I park the van there and he says I can camp on his ground. I carry a small battery charger and can hook it up and plug it into his power and burn my twelve volt lights and chargers. He's got a frost free hydrant I can draw water from, and a shower he says he'll loan me when needed.

Before leaving the van I dig into one of its hide-out compartments, grab a couple of small devices I might need, and pocket them.

The ARA canyon runs east and west and the first thing we do is take the road to their gate. There's not a gate house but there is a tent a hundred feet back in the trees. The white-haired guard, Craig Pasternak if I recall right, wanders out of the tent as we roar up and slide to a stop in front of the locked gate. Before he gets ten feet our way I have Hunter spin it around and haul ass. Hopefully he'll think we're just someone out for a joy ride.

Next we take a forest service road on the north side of the camp. I'm watching my GPS as we move a couple of miles back into the forest, and until I know we're a half-mile beyond the west border of the ARA property. Nowhere on that road did I have a visual of any of the camp buildings. But we have more luck on the south road, which is on a steeper slope, occasionally a sheer rock face. When we're at least three eighths of a mile from the camp, we stop and I break out my 60x Nikon spotting scope, and soon I'm surveying the camp below as if I'm only a hundred feet away.

A main building is about thirty by sixty feet with five smaller buildings scattered around in no particular order. They are each about twenty feet square, probably residential. There's also a barn and small corral fifty yards back up the canyon. All the buildings are chinked log structures, built long before ARA came on the scene, and all appear to have been re-roofed with brown metal. Each has its own stone fire-stack. Only a half-dozen vehicles are scattered around. One's a jeep much like Hunter's, only red where his is brown. Two white extended-length passenger vans probably seat ten or twelve each, and have ARA logos on their sides. The other three are passenger cars, one appearing to be a new Prius.

The camp is served by an electric line and by a propane tank of at least a thousand gallons.

It looks like at least three dogs are there, but as they lope along behind folks moving around, they appear to be pets—the largest being a black lab—not trained guard animals.

After I study the place for a few minutes, while Hunter sits on a log and smokes, he gets up and wanders over. "You got some kind of a hard-on for these folks or what?" I ignore him. "What's up?" he asks again.

"Just a run-away kid who got in with the wrong folks. Her folks want her home."

"Why not just walk in?"

"You know some of these guys. You think 'walk in' will get her out of there?"

He chuckles. "They are some kinds of assholes...different kind of bark-chewers than I've seen around. These guys act more like some paramilitary types."

"Then you know why. I want to spend another half hour here, checking things out, then I want to come back after dark. You okay with that?"

He shrugs. "You're paying by the hour."

Just as I'm about to fold up my tripod and put away my spotting scope I see two women stroll out of a cabin and head for the Prius.

I quickly put things up and instruct Hunter, "Looks like a couple of ladies are leaving the compound in a brown Prius. Let's see if we can beat them to the highway and tail along for a while."

"You da man," he says and has the Jeep fired up by the time I get my stuff put away.

He slides around a few curves on the way down, about runs over a whitetail deer, but makes Highway 1 just as the Prius passes, headed south-easterly toward Phillipsburg. As there's little traffic I have him stay a half-mile back. They're in no hurry, so it's a leisurely drive with a quiet oxbow Flint Creek on our right, meandering through a willow covered flat. It's turned out to be a beautiful late afternoon with a clear sky, no wind, and the smell of pines in the air. There's some kind of hatch on the creek and a few grasshoppers in the air, and the fish are making those little concentric rings on the surface that say "grab your fly rod," and I wish I could take time to do so.

The ladies swing the Prius into a gas station-restaurant-casino with a sign saying Sunshine Station, and I instruct Hunter to follow. They park and go inside and we go to the far side of the building, park, and enter through a restaurant that connects to the bar and casino they've entered.

We take a seat two stools down from the ladies, who turn out to be the illustrious mother superior, Maggie McFadden, tats and all, and a tall blond with perfectly straight hair to the small of her back and a thoroughbred racy body that says athlete, probably a runner. Maggie is dressed in jeans, a wide leather belt with spikes like a dog collar, and a green plaid flannel shirt and hiking boots. The blond has on black Lycra pants that would reveal every dimple in her butt, should she have any, and an un-tucked teal-blue silk blouse with the top buttons open to below ample boobs. It's pretty obvious she has on no bra—by the way they stand up she needs none—and tans sans clothing.

There's a line of poker and keno machines with the stools only feet to their back, so after I get my Jack Daniels from the doe eyed barmaid—who calls Hunter by name—and my change, I head to the machines, thinking I might be able to eavesdrop. The blond eyes me up and down as I slip onto a stool, and I give her a nod.

I can discern nothing from the look, so I ignore her and feed the machine. In moments I see that Hunter has slipped down the bar and is now next to Maggie. They're jawing away and the subject quickly turns to the bar fight at Maxville.

"Hey, Reardon," he calls and I spin on the stool. "This here's Maggie, and that's...what's your name?"

"Inga," the blond says.

"And that's Inga. They wanna meet the guy who cold-conked Mutt."

"Mutt?" I ask.

"The big ol' Indian boy you put down."

I laugh, then add, "I wasn't alone."

"What do you mean?" Hunter asks. I didn't see noboby over that'a'way."

"It was me and my buddy, Hickory."

"Hickory?" Maggie asks, and looks confused.

"I don't know—" Hunter begins.

"Hickory stick. I used a pool cue on him."

Hunter laughs, but Maggie gives me a frown.

"I knew it," she says. "He doesn't go down. We never heard of him being knocked down. Chicken shit to my way of thinking."

"Think whatever you want, sweetheart," I say, "however I'm still alive and a guy might not be he got hit by that buffalo."

This time she smiles. "Buy us a drink, we'll call it even, and won't tell Mutt you poleaxed him."

I don't want to act over eager, so I put them off a little. "I got a five in this machine. Soon as it's ten or a goose-egg, I'll join up."

I go ahead and bet four quarters a hand, lose four times in a row, and climb up on the stool on the other side of the blond. "Set 'em up," I say to the barmaid, draining what's left of my Jack.

"So, Inga, is it?" I ask her.

She bats her big green eyes and gives me a smile that might be a promise, but then quells it with, "Inga it is, but don't get any ideas, big boy. I'm committed."

"Oh, yeah, anybody I know?"

"Doubt it."

"Try me."

"You know Arne?"

I play dumb, even though I know exactly who she's talking about. Arnold 'Arne' Rostov, the stud-duck of ARA.

"You're right, I don't know him, so I wouldn't be crossing a friend when you and I slip out of here and find some hay to roll in."

Chapter Twelve

Inga laughs, and I like the sound of it. "You don't waste any time, do you?"

"Never saw the need, particularly when it comes to affairs of the heart."

This makes her laugh even harder. "Of the heart? I'd guess more like of the *hard*."

That makes me laugh, so I add, "A hard man is good to find."

"Got one, thanks."

I shrug. "Can't blame a fella for trying. I'll be around."

The barmaid has set the drinks down, so I pick mine up, toast her, and go back to my machine, but hear Maggie snarl "That's a real asshole. I'm gonna tell Arne about him."

"We don't need any more crap with the locals, besides, he's kinda cute," I hear Inga say, and she raises her voice a little so Hunter can hear. "Don't need trouble, do we, Manovitch?"

"None of us needs trouble," he says.

"I'm still telling Arne," Maggie grouses, "and he'll wanna beat some hide off this asshole."

I draw two more hands, then yell to Hunter, "Let's beat a trail."

He downs his drink, yells to the barmaid "See ya, Pet," and we head out. But I glance back as I push though the bar door in front, not the side door we came in, and she's lookin' back to see if I'm lookin' back to see and I am. She winks at me, I tip my hat, and we head out. Hunter gives me a curious look as I dig in my pocket, then bend and put a magnectic tracking device under the front bumper of the jeep. Then we're down the road and park where we can watch the Prius.

They couldn't have had more than one more drink when they exit and drive to Phillipburg's only grocery store, spend a half hour inside, and return with a half dozen bags and boxes full of groceries.

We hang back and follow until they make the turn into the ARA compound, then head for Maxville's Vet's bar for a burger and a beer. By nine-thirty, when the sun drops over the mountain, I head back to Hunter's place, park back in the trees, and unload my Harley so it's out of the way, and read some more of Pax's material before I turn off the light.

I've given up on visiting the ARA compound quite yet, as I'm still learning about the place and the folks there—and one of my reasons was to place some tracking devices in the cars, and I'm already one down.

Just as I'm about to hit the cot, a text comes through from Pax.

"What do you know about The Rocky Mountain Lab, Hamilton, Montana? Seems they study infectious disease and use lots of animals."

Chapter Thirteen

I immediately text him back, "Why do you ask?"

And almost as quickly receive "Pauly Rook, an ARA fanatic is a former employee, dismissed. Several ARA members have turned in applications there. Something is going on. Lab is a Nat. Institute Allergy and Infectious Disease facility. Some really BAD bugs there."

I reply "The Flot Phickens."

And get back "This one's no joke, pard. Watch these a-holes. I'm sending info."

And reply "Will do."

Interesting. Yes, I understand they use animals in their research, and that ARA would be concerned. But there's more to this ARA bullshit than appears on the surface. The more I study who's involved, and their backgrounds, the more I doubt a sincere concern with animals. Some of them, I'm sure, are sincere, but the top tier has another agenda and I'm going to discover what it is. Along, of course, with doing the job I've been retained to do.

The van has a tiny sink, an icebox, and a Porta-Potty. I also keep a propane camp stove and a few cans and packages of grub just in case there's no good old country cooking nearby. So I'm up with the sun, fire up the campstove, make myself some cowboy coffee and a bowl of instant oatmeal. As I keep a military cut, my hair takes little or no care, but I brush my snags and use a washcloth and a pot of water heated on my campstove for a spit bath and am halfway through it when my iPhone vibrates and I see there's a text message from Pax.

"I'm in two ARA computers—one's Rostov's personal and one seems an office type, used by lots of others. I'm getting blisters on my butt perched in front of mine. Sol can keep things rolling here. How about I come up?"

So I text back. "I haven't located the girl yet. Let's see how it goes. If we have to storm the ramparts I'll yell for help."

And he replies. "You sure you're not fly fishing?"

That makes me laugh. And I text back. "Not yet. Bring your rod if you come."

Sol is another computer genius and longtime employee of Pax's, a short dumpy kid with a brainpan the size of Texas.

"Guess what," he replies.

"Surprise me."

"Following the money. ARA has accounts at Wells Fargo in Missoula. Rostov has accounts in the Bahamas. Each time J. Remington has paid fifty grand to ARA, forty of it goes into Rostov's personal Bahama account."

That makes me smile. I wonder if J. J. knows where her money's going.

Pax is my best buddy. He and I served in Desert Storm together, both warrant officers, where he took an AK47 round through the thigh while saving my butt after a close RPG strike had me wandering around like a ten-martini drunk. He got out honorably, I got out with a general discharge as I took umbrage at some Haji men stoning a couple of young girls. That didn't fly with me,

71

but the lead did, and a half dozen of them went to their seventy virgin reward.

At six feet tall and two hundred twenty five hard pounds, Pax is just a couple of inches shorter than me and the same weight, and even with one leg now an inch and a half shorter than the other, he's hell on wheels and I'd rue the day we scrapped. He's also one of the finest marksmen to ever come down the pike, having competed in The Wimbledon Cup, the Marine Sniper School competition's 1,000 yard invitational, both while in the Corps and as an invitee thereafter. He never won, but he placed highly, and I don't want any of those guys drawing a bead on me even if I'm a mile away. Normal armed forces fire about fifteen thousand rounds for every kill…Marine snipers fire one point two rounds for every fatality.

It's said becoming a Marine sniper requires an awareness of the environment, total concentration, great woodsmanship, and a total disdain for the target. And I've watched Pax in action, and he's all of that and so much more.

He's also a computer guru, and has turned his Marine disability checks into an Internet Service Provider company with offices in Vegas and a half dozen other western cities. He's able to keep me under the radar, moving my money around through a dozen countries, adjusting my identity when necessary, and even obliterating records when propitious. He's a handy guy to have on your side, not to speak of the fact he's a hell of a good friend and we'd both get between a charging rhino and the other guy.

And his brother, Thornton, is a bail bondsman in L.A., and that's come in handy more than once, including the badge I carry as a bail enforcement officer.

I catch up on a little more reading and finish my third cup of coffee before Hunter wanders out of his cabin, stretching, hacking and coughing, then lighting up a smoke. I have a small folding chair and am enjoying the color up the canyon to the east, and to be truthful wish he'd slept longer.

"You wanna go get some chow?" he asks.

"I had a shot of lousy oatmeal, but yeah, I could use some real food. I want to be back before eight and I want you back up the road overlooking the camp. You take the spotting scope and write down everything that happens. Got it?"

"Don't sound too tough to me," he says, and coughs again, then asks, "So, what are you gonna do?"

"I'm gonna climb on my bike and stake out at the end of the road and follow anyone who wanders out. Eventually my girl might do so and if so I can have a chat with her."

"So I just flop down and watch—"

"And record everything that happens in that camp. We're going to start trying to identify all of them. If it's a girl, the tall blond we met for instance, then write down what building she came out of and where she went and what she did. If she, or he, is a roly-poly critter in shorts and spike hair, write that down…got it?"

"I can handle it."

"Good. Where are we going to eat?"

"We can go back to the Sunshine Station, the other way to Drummond where they's a couple of joints, or to

Hall where they's a place…if it's open. It kinda comes and goes."

"Which is closest?"

"Hall, I'd guess."

"Then let's haul, if you'll pardon the pun."

"What's a pun?"

"Let's go eat. I'm riding my Harley. I'll follow you."

He shrugs, and heads for his jeep.

I'm not the most patient guy in the world, and it's time I make something happen. If she doesn't come out, I'm going in.

Chapter Fourteen

During breakfast I learn some things about my new employee. Hunter's real first name is Harley, as was his father, whom he hates as he abandoned the family when Hunter was a toddler. Thus the name change, of his own volition. Hunter not only works as a sawyer, but is a trapper in the winter, so he has some real backwoods skills. He was raised on the highline, the part of northern Montana up against the Canadian border, in a town that holds the national record for the greatest change in temperature in a single day. Cutbank, Montana went from eighty degrees to twenty below in one twenty-four hour period, a one hundred degree drop. It pays to keep a coat in your truck in Montana…even in July.

Hunter worked as a cowboy, a logger, a trucker, and was a soldier serving in a construction unit for one tour of duty, all stateside. He still sends money to his mama in Cutbank, every month, as she's an asthmatic and can't work.

I'm gaining a new respect for the ol' boy.

We return to our assignments for the day, Hunter up on the forest service road overlooking the ARA compound, me sitting on my Harley Iron backed into the trees a hundred yards north from the mouth of the access road to the camp. I'm there before eight, and spend some time on my email on my iPhone, reviewing what turns out to be junk mail…until I glance up to see a four door Jeep Rubicon, steel gray and tricked out with powerful lights mounted on the top, a winch that looks big enough to lift the unit up a tree, and a breather so it can run in deep water. It's a real man's rig, but it turns my way and as it passes I see it's loaded with ladies. Two girls in the front, two in the back. I let it get a half-mile down the road, then fire up and follow.

I figure they're on the way to the market in Drummond, but instead they take Highway 90 west toward Missoula. A ladies day on the town?

It's about fifty miles from Drummond to Missoula, if that's where they're heading, so I settle in for a nice long ride then close the distance between us as we near town. As I suspected, they turn off on the third ramp, Orange Street, and are held up by traffic. Luckily, there's a big rig between us, and I stay difficult to spot. The Jeep is pretty distinctive so I can hold back, staying over a block behind. As I might suspect from a group of women, they head straight for the mall. I'm only a hundred yards from them when they park near Dillard's, one of the Mall's anchor stores, and unload.

I've passed through Missoula only once before. It's a picturesque university town of some fifty thousand on the very north end of the Bitterroot Valley, one of Montana's fastest growing areas. Sandwiched between the Sapphire Mountains to the east and the magnificent Bitterroot-Selway Mountains to the west, it's a forty-five mile long valley of cattle ranches and yuppie gentleman farmer ten-acre parcels, spotted with a few small towns. The Bitterroot River winds down the valley, flowing south to north, between groves of willows and cottonwood, peppered with the occasional copse of Ponderosa, fir, and lodgepole pine. The crest of the Bitterroots is the dividing line between Montana and Idaho's panhandle.

The blond I met in Phillipsburg—Inga—is driving. Next to her in the front is Maggie McFadden, stringy gray hair, tats and all. Out of the back unlimbers a tall rather attractive redhead with short cropped hair and a rather dumpy dirty blond who, I have high hopes, is my target, Jane Jasper Remington. J. J.'s hair is pulled back, not like the pictures I have, so I'll need to get closer to confirm her identity. A one and a half inch butterfly tat on the back of her neck will be absolute confirmation. They head straight for the glass doors leading into the big department store, and I follow at a discreet distance. All but McFadden are dressed in sports clothes, clean and sharp. The blond, Inga, even wears low heels. Maggie's in jeans and a stretched out tee shirt, wearing unattractive Birkenstocks that have seen better days.

I let them get in the place before I lock my helmet to the bike with a bike cable, then make a pass by the Jeep and stick a tracking device under the steel back bumper. As I wander toward the entrance I text Pax with the vehicle's license number and description and the I.D. number of the tracking device. Two ARA vehicles will now go nowhere that we don't know about.

Following them at a distance, which is hard to do in a department store, I get the impression that Maggie is more the chaperone, maybe even guard, than a participant in the girl's day out. She stays alert, eyes cutting this way and that, and never once fingers a blouse, or purse, or piece of costume jewelry. I do get a glance, over a rack of Calvin Klein rags, of a butterfly tat on the back on the dirty blond,s neck. Maybe it's a good thing she's wearing her hair up.

I watch for an opportunity to have a word with J. J., but the girls stay close together. Finally, with only a couple of small shopping bags between them, they wander out into the mall and make their way in and out of several shoe and dress shops. I'm able to take a seat in a rest area in the center of the mall and track them visually as they duck in and out of stores. I do this for almost three hours, while I consume two cups of coffee, visit the head once, and catch up on my texts and email. Women can shop. They finally enter a Red Robin where I presume they are having lunch. I take a table across the room, and I avoid Inga's green eyed glance, then her stare. I think I'm made, but it should make no difference.

They order about the same time I do, then Inga, again giving me the eye, rises as if she might be heading over to say howdy. An instance after she stands, I jump up and head for the john, and out of the side of my vision see her hesitate, then return to her seat.

She says something to Maggie, who stares after me, but sort of shrugs and doesn't get up to follow.

As luck sometimes smiles on me, as I'm leaving the men's room, J. J. Remington is heading for the ladies and I run into her, out of sight of the table full of her compatriots.

"J. J." I say, and she stops and gives me a curious look.

"Do I know you?" she asks, a little bit of a coy smile like she might like to know me.

"I'm a family friend," I reply, and her smile fades.

"A family friend of my father's. Forget it." And she tries to brush past me.

As gently as I can without being too insistent, I stop her with a hand on her upper arm. "Yes, I'm a friend of your father's…a paid consultant, actually. Are you aware that Rostov has been banking money you've given ARA into his personal account in the Bahamas?"

Her face goes blank, and she hesitates a moment. "How would you know that, even if it's true?"

"My people are very industrious."

"Well, it doesn't matter. If Arne did it, it's fine and for the cause."

"His cause," I say.

"Leave me alone," she says, and jerks away, and I let her go. It would be less than wise to drag a young woman out of a public place. I turn to head back to my table and find myself face to face with Maggie McFadden.

"Who the fuck are you?" she snaps.

"Don't you remember, Miss Maggie, we met at the Sunshine Station."

"Fuck yes, I remember, but that's not the question, asshole. Who are you, and what do you want?"

"I want to eat my lunch." I give her my most winning smile. I guess it's not winning enough.

"We'll eat your fucking lunch…and you, you don't stay the fuck away from us."

"Oh, who's us?"

"ARA."

"What the fuck is an ARA?" I reply in my most innocent tone but deciding to get into the flow of her vernacular.

"Just stay away from me and my girls. We see you again, you might just get fucked up."

I shrug, and laugh a little as I offer, "I've been fucked up most my life, sunshine, and to be truthful, getting fucked up, down, or around by you just isn't on my agenda," and brush past her and head back to my table. I guess that leaves her a little speechless as no expletives follow me.

She waits until J. J. exits the ladies room then escorts her back to their table. I can tell by the expressions and body language that Maggie is grilling J. J. as they walk, and if I read it right, J. J. is not giving her any info. It seems she might not want ARA to know that her father is on the hunt for her. I get only one quick glance from J. J. before she reaches her table, and give her a wink, which I don't know if she sees. But she sure as hell doesn't wink back. Her brow is furrowed.

As I'm made, I decide to leave before they do and gobble my burger and fries down and head out. Since I'm halfway there, I decide to take a ride up the Bitterroot Valley to Hamilton and check out the Rocky Mountain Lab. If it's a place of interest to ARA, it's a place of interest to me.

Besides, who wouldn't want to know where some of the world's most deadly critters live? Critters that can wipe out the entire population of this planet, should they be loosed upon it.

Chapter Fifteen

Highway 93 bisects the long Bitterroot Valley, as does the Bitterroot River. It's a great ride on my Iron, passing through or by Lolo, Florence, Stevensville, Victor and Corvallis before crossing the river just before Highway 93 becomes the city street North 1st, which becomes South 1st when it crosses Main Street.

I hang a right onto Main, which is just a little over three blocks of businesses, see a café on the south side and flip a U turn and back my Harley into the angled parking. I've passed a couple of likely looking saloons on the way in, and may sneak back there after I get the coffee drinkers take on things. Unfortunately, the Signal Grill doesn't have a counter, only tables, and there's only one other customer—a fugitive from Duck Dynasty—in the middle of the day. He's having what looks like berry pie and coffee, with only a few crumbs hung up in his gray beard, so I take a table next to him and strike up a conversation.

"The pie worth a try? Is that blackberry?"

"It's huckleberry, and if you ain't tried it you ain't lived."

I laugh and look over my shoulder to see a waitress with askew black hair, Coke bottle bottom glasses, supp-hose, practical black crepe soled shoes, and a smile that seems a sincere welcome.

She rates a smile. "I'll have that pie, and a couple of dips of ice cream."

"You want it heated?" she asks.

"You decide."

"Heated," the old boy says.

"Thanks. You farm around here?" The overalls and the well-worn gloves stuffed into his back pocket have probably already answered the question.

"Yep, a little alfalfa and raise some black angus."

"Cattle price good?"

"Never good enough. We get a buck a pound and feed prices take it back. You not from around here?"

"No, sir, thinking about looking for work. I hear there's a big lab around here that might be hiring."

He gives a "humph," and eyes me up and down. "You don't look like no lab rat."

"I figure they might need some maintenance types or janitorial…or hell, I've done security work. What I hear about what they grow, they probably have lots of security?"

"Yep, lots. I wouldn't work there for all the tea in China."

I laugh. "That's lots of tea."

The waitress arrives in time to add "Won't do you no good if you're dead."

As she places the pie and ice cream in front of me, I ask, "So, they have lots of accidents?"

The old man answers, "I been here seventy years and they was here when I was growin' up, and as far as I know, they never had no accidents. How-some-ever, when they do it'll probably be a doosey."

He's right about the pie, so I ask for a cup of coffee and she hurries away. I turn back to the old man. "So, you wouldn't work there?"

"Damn place sounds like a jet plane going over half the time. Neighbors have been complaining about the sound since they blew seventy million of the taxpayer's money on a new building...even built a moat around the place."

My mouth is full of pie and ice cream, so it's a moment before I can ask, "A moat? They afraid of the locals storming the ramparts?"

"Nope, they say ticks can't swim."

"Ticks?"

"Yea, among the many other things...ebola, spotted fever, flu...they study that Lyme disease, and use lots of ticks."

"I worked for a vet for a couple of years and handled lots of small animals. They use critters?"

"Yep, rats, rabbits, ferrets and monkeys. Ever time I see a rabbit I jump five feet...but they claim nothing ever got away."

"Well, you've convinced me, I'm not looking for work there."

"Smart young fella. You ever buck hay?"

"Yes, sir, all I want to buck."

He looks a little disappointed and goes back to his pie. I finish mine before him, check the ticket the girl's left on the table, leave her a two-buck tip, and head out. Before I fire up the bike, I check Safari on my iPhone and get a location of the lab. To my surprise, it's short of the river to the west and right up against a residential area on the southwast corner of town.

One would think a place like that would be in the middle of lonely…like maybe the Sahara Desert.

The complex of buildings, probably fifty or sixty acres of fenced structures, looks to be over a hundred thousand square feet under roof, none over two stories. It's well fenced, and a guard house protects the entrance, flanked by in-and-out lanes. As I pass, innocently enough except for looking a little like a Hell's Angel, I note the guard keeps his eyes on me. Three sides of the complex are bordered by residences, and the fourth side backs up to the cottonwood covered riparian area of the river, which appears to have changed its course several times over the years.

You can't completely circle the place, so I retrace my path, and again note that the uniformed guard observes me closely. I wave, but unlike most Montana residents, he doesn't wave back. His gaze, under a black bill cap, is penetrating. I think these guards are serious, and thank God for it.

I've seen enough for the time being, and not liking to retrace my steps, decide to take the Skalkaho highway back to Phillipsburg. I know it's dirt most of the way as I've quizzed Hunter about alternate areas away from Maxville where I'm camped, and away from the ARA compound as I may want to leave in a hurry some time in the future.

Only in Montana, or maybe in my home state of Wyoming, would a dirt road be called a highway. And few other places would have such a beautiful highway to travel. The Skalkaho takes off from Highway 93 just south of Hamilton, heading east into the Sapphire Mountains and then between them and the Pintler Range. It's only about 45 miles back in lieu of the hundred I came, but it's dirt most of the way, and closed in the winter.

I'm immediately happy I took the wild way home, spotting a bald eagle, several ospreys, and a cow elk and her calf as well as several mule deer and a few whitetail along the creek. The mountains to the south, the Pintlers, climb to ten thousand feet and are still snow covered on the peaks, with some long creek bottom valleys lined with willows leading up into them. I stop and watch a Shira moose, only fifty yards off the road, a young bull with about a two-foot horn spread. He's grazing the bottom of a beaver pond. He gives me a long look like he's considering breeding my Harley, but then goes back to grazing, water and moss dripping from his mouth.

By the time I reach Highway One, after taking a turn and following the East Fork of Rock Creek, I'm only a mile or so from Sunshine Station...and it's cocktail time. I call Hunter, who picks up on the first ring.

"I'm headed for the Sunshine Station," I inform him. "You still on the job?"

"Yep, and I've about run out of ink. This is a busy place. Two other carloads of hippies have arrived. Nine more bark chewers are on the scene."

"Is there any reason to stay longer?"

"Nope, there's a damn good reason to get the hell out of here and have a beer."

"You sure?" I ask.

"Damn sure. Those boys have unloaded a dozen or more what looks like AR15's. Are these guys planning a war?"

Chapter Sixteen

Dark comes late in Montana summers and it's still light when Hunter and I have finished a couple of beers and a plateful of chicken fried steak, mashed potatoes, gravy, and buttered corn. I've reviewed Hunter's notes and, yes, it was a busy day around the ARA compound. Part of that 'busy' was a couple of new vehicles, a Ford pickup with a cover on the back and a brand new Toyota Highlander seating eight, and eight were therein as well as three in the pickup, all men, all looking more like they'd chew nails than bark.

I'm about to order a piece of pie and compare the Sunshine Station's to the Hamilton café's, when my phone does a few notes of *Ring of Fire* and I know it's Pax.

He seldom bothers with hello, and this is no exception. "They're on the move."

"Both marked cars?"

"Both, just turned out of the access road and are headed north on Highway 1."

"I'll get on my horse," I say, and wave the waitress over—Pet I've learned is her name—indicating I want a check.

"I want to come up," Pax grouses.

"Hold on." I turn to Hunter who's gnawing his last bite of chicken fried. "You want to keep working?"

"Why not. I was supposed to take sweet Al to the movie, but her relief didn't show so she's got to close up."

I turn back to the phone. "I had a few words with the daughter at lunch time, and I don't think I'm going to be able to talk her out of there...so come on up. We also have more ARA types on the scene, who arrived with enough fire-power to start a small insurrection."

"I'll text you my travel arrangements."

Hunter has his Jeep but I want to stay on the job with my van, and possibly some of what's hidden in his hide-out panels. I lead the way and swing off through Maxville, trade Harley Iron for Van, and quickly apply some magnetic signs to each side of the van. Now I'm Alliance Plumbing and Sheet Metal. And we're back on the road.

As I knew he would, Pax continues to text me with the movements of the tracking devices. Both vehicles still together, now having turned west on Highway 90 toward Missoula. Looks like I get another visit to the university town.

Hunter and I both have our cell phones, and both have Motorola hand-helds, so we're able to stay in touch. By the time I again take the Orange Street turnoff, Pax tells me we're only a half mile or so behind the tracking devices, which are following the same route I did earlier in the day.

I'm wondering if they're not on their way to some kind of move on the Rocky Mountain Lab, and maybe if we should have a pair of Hazmat suits.

My phone buzzes with a text, and Pax informs me they've stopped, both at the same place, which allows Hunter and me to close the distance between us and them. Just as we reach where they've stopped, I see Maggie exiting a service station mini-market, carrying a couple of cups of coffee. Both the Prius and the Jeep Rubicon are gassing up. A Ford pickup with a cover on the back and the Toyota Highlander are on the lot and Maggie is talking to guys in two other vehicles. It seems most of the ARA camp is on the move. There are at least a dozen men and three or four women. Then I see J. J., my target, exit the market's exterior ladies room door and pile into a vehicle. It's just getting dark, but J. J. is well lit by the mini-market's lights.

Four vehicles: the Prius, the Rubicon, the Toyota and the Ford. Something big is up. I don't think they're taking in dinner and a movie, particularly since they're all dressed in black.

And they head out north, taking Highway 93 toward Hamilton, the home of Rocky Mountain Lab.

We follow at a discreet distance. Then, to my slight surprise, they turn back east, toward the little town of Stevensville, pass through it, and suddenly we're out in a sparsely populated area in the foothills of the Sapphire Mountains. I let Hunter in the Jeep lead the way and kill the lights on the van, not wanting it to look like a platoon is following the ARA vehicles. Then he suddenly pulls off to the side and kills his lights as I realize the four vehicles have slowed almost to a stop.

Hunter walks back to the van and leans on the driver's side door. "Did you notice the sign back there?"

"I missed it."

"Funky Furs. One of the biggest mink growers in Montana is just up ahead. I'll bet the ARA types are up to some old tricks."

I sigh, wondering just what the hell we should do. I'm not here to protect some fur farm's investment, but then again I'm not real happy with what I've observed about ARA. Are they really what they claim—animal rights advocates—or something more? Right now it looks like animal rights advocates is right on the money.

The four ARA vehicles have disappeared from sight, probably having turned their lights off.

I text Pax with the company name, and almost as quickly I get a Google Earth aerial of Funky Farms and a report that the two tracking devices have stopped on the far side of Funky Furs.

I dig a Smith and Wesson M&P15 out of one of the hideout panels in the van and a pair of night vision goggles, pull the van well off the road, lock it up, and join Hunter in his jeep.

He eyes the .223 and stutters a little, "We...uh...we going to war?"

"Nope, just being cautious. There's a road on the property this side of the fur farm, and it's the high ground. Let's wander up there, lights off. I'd like to observe for a while."

But he's not quite convinced. "I ain't ready for no shooting war."

"Nor am I...but you said they had a pile of weapons and I don't want to take a smile to a gunfight. We're gonna stay out of their way. I just want to watch...."

He shrugs, fires up the Jeep, leaves the lights off, and in moments we're atop a small hill on the west side of Funky Furs, less than a quarter mile from what appears to be a house—dark, no lights—with a walkway connected to an office-fronted barn at least eighty feet in length. There's a two car garage next to the house, but the garage doors are open and no vehicles are parked inside. A silo, probably full of feed, is next to the barn. A small vacation trailer, maybe twenty feet in length, sits behind the barn, and it has lights on and a mini-truck parked in front. The place appears to be a forty-acre parcel, nicely treed, and almost covered with raised cages to about the height of a man.

I keep scanning the area with the night-vision glasses. Then I realize that three men are approaching the trailer, all carrying long arms. In moments they bust in and drag a man out, and shove him to his knees, two keeping him covered while a third binds his hands behind him and his ankles. They shove him over, then I see a dozen other ARA types charge into the rows of cages and begin ripping paperwork off the front of the cages and opening cage doors.

That's of interest to me, but no more than the fact that two blackclad men carrying long arms are breaking into the darkened house. One of them also carries a sledge hammer and the other a big crow bar. They kick the back door in, and lights come on inside. I have a clear view through a wide sliding glass door into what appears to be a master bedroom, and see them go straight to a framed picture on the wall, tear it away and discard it, then begin ripping a wall safe right out of the wall. Within ten minutes they're back outside and heading away, one of them now carrying the safe, the other carrying both weapons. I guess they've left their tools behind.

In twenty minutes, they've stolen the safe, opened most if not all the cages, and have escaped.

I have Hunter drive me back to the van, and on the way get a text from Pax that the marked vehicles are heading north, back toward Missoula, on a back road.

I pull a throwaway cell phone out of the van's glove compartment, make a quick call to 911 and report lots of cars and suspicious activity at Funky Furs, then haul ass. I'm feeling guilty about not going down and freeing the Funky Fur employee, or night watchman, or whatever he is and hope he's okay…but I'm not ready to explain to the local sheriff why I was perched on a nearby hill with night vision equipment and a fully automatic M&P15 with two 30 round clips taped together.

I'm heading home to Maxville.

I'll read about it in the newspaper tomorrow, and hope the guy tied up on the ground doesn't get eaten by a bevy of pissed off minks.

Chapter Seventeen

Hunter headed out to have breakfast with Al, his girlfriend, with instructions to take his notebook and my spotting scope back to the mountainside and spend the day doing recon.

I'm shocked when I go to breakfast in Drummond at The Wagon Wheel, pick up a *Missoulian* newspaper, and read that eco-terriorists have stolen a half million dollars in cash, gold coins, and diamonds and murdered the son of the Funky Furs owners near Stevensville.

Not only shocked, but saddened and angry to the marrow of my bones. I can feel the heat creep up my backbone and know that if I let it settle in my brain, I'll roar into the ARA compound and do my best to dispatch every male there, as I'm sure it was men who dragged the kid out of his trailer and then broke into the house and made off with the wall safe.

I guess I missed the fact that they not only tied the kid up—a kid who was only seventeen—but slit his throat.

And I stood on my hilltop and watched, and did nothing. I feel like I should go in the bathroom and puke.

As I've thought since I met with Remington in NY, these guys have ulterior motives for their supposed animal rights activities. A half million is certainly an ulterior motive.

One would wonder why a guy would keep a half million in cash, gold and diamonds in his bedroom wall safe, but when you consider the obscene low interest rates banks pay on savings deposits, it becomes somewhat more clear. In fact I'm surprised most folks aren't burying their savings in their back yard. And the article relates that Mr. Allenthorpe, owner of Funky Furs, often traded furs for gold and diamonds.

The Allenthorpes, as the article reveals, came home to find their cages open and animals in the wild, all the breeding records—the paperwork was on the front of each cage—destroyed. And, far worse, their son murdered. At least I called 911 and the sheriff was waiting there when they arrived, their son covered with a tarp.

Fuck.

I'm picking Pax up at the Missoula airport at noon, and am glad of it, as he's always a calming influence. I, on the other hand, rush in where angels fear to tread. I know he'll bring me to my senses and not only see that I do the job I'm hired to do, but make sure I stay clear of the cold blooded murder charges I'd so like to incur at the moment.

I need to get the other ARA vehicles marked with a tracking device. I need to listen in on some private conversations between Rostov, Hutchins, McFadden and the others at the top rung of the dirty ladder.

I've made up my mind that I'm not only going to do my job—recovering Remington's daughter—but I'm going to clean up this rat's nest.

The hell of it is, part of this bunch are kids with good, if misguided, hearts and intentions. The last thing I want is to punish the wrong ARA member. I'll probably know a lot more soon as Pax says he's bringing a ream of material on ARA members, this time from the bottom up as he was able to recover a file full of pledges—wherein all members have signed and pledged to support and be faithful to the group, and to all animals of the universe. I have to laugh and wonder if they've ever come face to face with a spitting cobra.

And again I laugh as they've all pledged their personal possessions and net worth to the support of the organization and its aims. I wonder how many of them know about Rostov's growing Bahama bank account?

I have time to calm down a little on the fifty mile drive from Drummond to Missoula, only to find that Pax's flight's been delayed over an hour due to some mechanical problem. So I return a couple of miles to town, find a Sportsman's Warehouse, and invest a couple of hundred bucks in 9mm, 7.62 and .223 ammo, then find an REI store and invest a couple of hundred more in some climbing gear just for the hell of it. Actually, some of the country flanking the ARA compound would require ropes and pitons to scale.

This time the plane arrives and I'm happy to note Pax has not eaten, as it's past lunch time and Hunter has suggested I try The Montana Club, just off Highway 90 on the same drag, Reserve Street, where I found both stores.

Pax, never one to waste much time, hauls in a two inch binder stuffed with info on ARA members, and I read while he tries to make time with a cute waitress, to no avail.

Of note is the fact that Jane Jasper Remington is not the only trust fund baby to become a disciple of the Animal Revolutionary Army. Four other girls, all in their late teens and early twenties, are all former members of the Animal Liberation Army, the Animal Rights Militia, or Animals NOW. And all the girls are from very wealthy families who've foolishly set them upon the world with sizable assets in their own names, and no blisters from having earned a dime of it. It's a bad combination, particularly when you have a warped sense of who's on top, man or animal. I love animals, particularly dogs and horses, but if I have to choose between an animal and a parent, or any other human being, there's no question in my mind what the choice has to be. No question.

When our food comes, I look up from my reading and ask, "So, what's not in this pile?"

He smiles. "They've been doing quite a lot of emailing, even back and forth among themselves, much of it encoded. I have Sol working on it now. Probably by the time we're back to your camp site he'll have a pile of decoded messages. What's next on your plate?"

"I want to get some trackers on the other vehicles and a listening device or two in place. There's a meeting room we need to bug and Rostov's personal quarters."

"So, we have a date there tonight?"

"You have a date with my SASS."

"Great, you picked up another one?"

"Yep, semi-auto, XM110, 7.62 in the case with night vision and a 6 x 20 Nikon that looks good. You'll be able to put one through an eyeball at a half mile. Let's get the hell out of here so we can sight it in on the way back."

"Over the counter, I hope?" he asks, with a tight grin.

"Over a pickup tailgate. I didn't ask where he got it and he didn't ask why I wanted it. He was smiling when he left with six grand in his jeans."

Just as we get back to the van, my phone vibrates in my pocket. I glance as I bring it out, Hunter.

"Hey," he begins, "they're on the move again."

Chapter Eighteen

I cover the phone with a hand and ask Pax, "Can you track the ARA vehicles with your laptop?"

"Does a big bear ka ka in these here hills?"

I go back to the phone. "Can you trail them in your jeep without getting spotted?"

"Shit yeah," he says, and I wish I was so confident.

"We're headed your way. Keep in touch on the phone. How many cars?"

"Looks like six this time. Must be thirty or more of them."

"Is the girl with them?"

"Hell if I know. Lot's of them is girls."

"You gonna be able to tell which way they've gone?"

"I doubt if I'll get down to the highway in time."

"We'll track the Prius and the Rubicon and call you when we know which way they turn."

"Ten four," he replies, and is gone.

"Thanks, Alysia," Pax says, leaving the cute waitress a ten dollar tip, which gets him a smile and a wave.

I filled Pax in on the events at Funky Furs while we ate and as we headed back east on Highway 90, and while he sets up his laptop to track the Prius and Rubicon, he quizzes me.

"Why didn't you turn these ARA a-holes over to the local law?"

"First, I didn't realize they'd sliced the kid's throat. I thought they'd left him tied up. Second, if I did it and the locals busted them it would take a year to get the pricks to trial, even in Montana, and then they might get life in the can which I think is real injustice. Worse, some of the bad guys might get to walk. The kid rots in a grave, his family mourns for the rest of their lives and are never happy again, and the rotten cocksuckers get three hots and a cot and TV and a weight room. No way. I may get a chance to be judge, jury, and executioner…and that's just fine by me. I'll deal with them when I know for sure who goes down for the count. I'll deal with the pearly gates when it's my time."

Pax chuckles. "Well, you haven't mellowed much. I get it, believe me." He plays with the keys a moment, then I can hear the smile in his voice. "I've got them on screen. They're passing Phillipsburg, heading southeast. What's that way?"

"Don't know, haven't been that way. I should have put a tracker on Hunter's Jeep so we'd know where he is in case he gets out of phone range."

I pick up my iPhone and poke Hunter's number in.

"What direction?" he answers.

"They're headed past Phillipsburg. Any idea where they might be going?"

"Hell, Georgetown Lake, or Anaconda, or any of a hundred campgrounds. Nothing that way in the way of animal farms or whatnot that I know of."

"Get on their tail if you can catch up."

Hell, maybe they're out for a day's fun after their great success at Funky Furs?

So I turn to Pax. "If all, or even most of them are gone, this will give us a chance to bug the compound."

"And miss what they're up to?" Pax says.

"I want to make sure who the real bad guys are. I don't want to put down some innocent kid who's been hoodwinked by Rostov and his cronies. And I don't want to have to kidnap Jane Jasper. I'd have to drive her all the way to New York and then worry about her filing charges no matter what her old man says."

"Let's see who they left behind, if anyone."

"Oh, there'll be someone standing guard."

Rather than head straight for ARA's camp, I return to Hunter's cabin, mount up on the Harley, and get a Glock for Pax. He follows me back to the turn off to the ARA compound and we make a plan. He changes clothes into hiking attire, concealing the Glock in the small of his back under his un-tucked shirt. He'll leave the van out of sight of the gate and go to the gate on foot, a lost hiker, and if there's a guard he'll keep him busy while I slip down the mountain and plant a few devices. I'm going up the forest service road overlooking the compound with my binocs and will drop down as close as I can get and still see the gate.

We'll both have our handheld Motorola radios and he'll leave his in transmit mode in his shirt pocket while talking to the guard, if any, and I'm sure there will be. I'll be able to hear what's going on. We also have cell phones.

We normally wouldn't do this in daylight, but I'm sure most—maybe all—are out of the camp.

The last thing I do before we part is call Hunter again. "What's up?"

"They went on past the lake, heading toward Anaconda."

"You managing to stay out of sight?"

"I'm staying way back. Hard to miss a half dozen vehicles."

"You call me if they turn around and head back this way. I'm paying a visit to their camp."

"Will do."

I'm pleased the Harley has a good muffler as I have to gun it a couple of times on the steep mountain road, then up a slope to hide her in a thick copse of lodgepole pine. I have a small backpack full of gear, and slip and slide my way down the mountainside, then stop short as I come upon a half dozen half-inch thick black rubber irrigation lines.

Strange. Out of place on a mountainside. I follow them uphill a ways and discover they are being fed by a small spring, then turn and follow them back down past the place I discovered them, still three hundred yards from and above the camp.

It doesn't take long before I come upon a five foot by fifty foot graded flat spot, and a hundred full grown and budding marijuana plants, being watered by one of the lines. I follow on to a second, and presume the other three lines lead to more patches.

But Pax should be nearing the gate, so I hustle down closer to the camp until I reach a spot where I can see the gate through the trees. And I'm just in time, as he's wandering up, doing a good imitation of a lost hiker. From a small wall-tent gatehouse fifty feet back from the locked gate, a tall, gangly, white haired guy hustles out, carrying an AR15 loosely in a hand hanging at his side.

He stops five feet back from the gate, and I fit an earpiece in and turn up the volume.

"This is private property," I hear a voice challenge.

Chapter Nineteen

"Sorry, am I trespassing?" Pax asks, and even from four hundred yards, through my binocs, I can see the silly grin on his face.

"As soon as you got off the highway you were trespassing," the guy snaps.

"Sorry, again. My map must be wrong. It says this is Forest Service on this side of your gate."

"You can't believe them fucking maps," the guy growls, and lies.

The wide vehicle gate is wrought iron, with six-inch gaps, and Pax shoves his hand through to shake. I watch long enough to laugh as I hear him introduce himself, "I'm Ferral Nightengale. Nice to meet you."

I'd like to stay and be entertained, but I have to move in order to cross an open area while the gate guy is busy looking the other way. And I do, hauling ass until I'm up beside the main log building, out of sight of the gate. I find an unlocked side door, peek in to see there's no one in the large meeting area, then hustle to a podium in front of a dozen tables and fit a transmitting device under a lip of the slanted oak top and a matchbox size video camera in a potted fern on a fern stand in a corner where it can cover most the room. It'll only transmit a hundred yards or so, but it's motion and noise activated and will set idle for days until it senses someone nearby. Hunter has Rostov's cabin delineated—the last one, and the largest one, among the buildings. I haul ass for it at the back of the property.

There are only a couple of vehicles on the property, except for a bike—a Honda rice-burner VFR800 V-Tec—parked in a small covered carport on the side of his pad. Could he be home?

There's one way to find out, and I bang on the door. And hear noise inside. Uh oh!

"Hold on," a voice calls out...a feminine voice.

The door swings aside and, even under the circumstances, I have to smile. Inga Sorrensen, with lots of smooth tan flesh showing over and under tight short-shorts and a bikini top.

Her emerald green eyes widen. "How did you get in?"

"I was hiking, and dropped down the mountain from over there," I point up the opposite mountainside from where the Harley is hidden.

"That's a pile," she says. "You just happened to wander up to my door while my boyfriend is away?" Her smile is a little devilish, and I like it. I can't help but let my eyes wander up and down her beach-brown, very luscious body from crimson painted toenails to red plastic hair clip.

"God helps those who help themselves," I say, and give her my most devilish smile in return. "So, am I invited in?"

"He'll kill you, and probably me, if he finds you here."

"God, or your boyfriend? Doesn't matter...there are just some things worth dying for," I say, and go ahead and shove my way inside. "So, when's the luckiest guy in Montana due back?"

She laughs, and walks over to a cabinet and gets two glasses and a bottle of Wild Turkey. "Late. Everyone went to dinner over in Anaconda. There's a great steakhouse there if you haven't been. I presume you drink?"

"Only good whiskey, like Turkey."

She pours three fingers in each glass, pads across the floor in bare feet, and hands me one. I drop the backpack off, hanging in one hand at my side. "Here's to new friends," she toasts.

"With benefits, I hope. And to boyfriends foolish enough to leave a beautiful woman...already half-undressed...home alone."

She smiles again, and takes a hard slug on the booze.

I drink too.

She takes a step closer. "He's mad at me because I said I'm leaving."

"Well, hell, let's give him a reason to be really pissed off." And I lean down and nibble a pouty lip, as she leans her head back, offering me both lips which I take in a kiss that keeps getting deeper, and hotter, until I've backed her to an interior door that I presume is a bedroom.

The bikini top is tied in a bow behind her neck, and I drop the backpack to the bedroom floor as I continue to kiss her, and untie the top and back away just far enough so it falls exposing a pair of flawlessly tanned perfect 36 d's with pebble hard nipples begging to be suckled, and as I push her down on the bed and nibble my way down her throat and over her shoulder to a hard nipple...someone bangs on the door.

My growing erection turns to worm as I leap up.

She's past me like a streak, tying the bikini as she goes. I close the door behind her, open my backpack, stick a transmitter under the drawer of a bedside table, and head for a rear door.

I'm gone, headed for the hillside and the cover of the brush, rocks, and trees. As soon as I gain fifty feet up—finding it hard to climb with blue balls—I find the cover of a rock pile and watch to see the white-haired guard staring up my way, then walking away from the front door of Rostov's cabin.

It's all I can do not to head back down, but my initial job is done, and the job I was taking on will have to wait...goddamn the piss poor luck.

I hit the vibrate button on the little radio, and only one word comes back, and it's whispered, "Go."

"You clear," I ask Pax.

"Clear, back at the van and firing it up. How'd it go?"

I laugh. "You won't believe it. See you back at the cabin...or better yet, stop at the Vet's Hall on the way by and I'll treat you to a beer."

"Ten four," he replies, and I climb on up to the Harley, fire it up, and head for Maxwell's only bar.

He beats me there by a few minutes, and is already charming Al right out of her socks. The bar is vacant except for the two of them. She's giggling like an eighth grader when I join him at the bar. "A beer," I ask, "if you can break away from this charming conversation?" She walks to the end to draw one from the tapper and I turn to Pax. "That's a buddy's woman, buddy," I chastise him.

"A better buddy than me?" he asks.

"Maybe a better shot," I suggest.

"Doubt the hell out of that," he says, with a chuckle.

"Me too, but leave her alone anyhow."

"Since when is it against the law to charm the natives?"

"It's not, but he's turning out to be a pretty good guy. Ex-Army, but we won't hold it against him. So, speaking of better shot, when are we gonna sight in the SASS?"

"Probably not after six beers. Are the hamburgers any good here?"

"Fat and sassy, a little like charming Al."

"Good, then I'll have one, or two, after we have a few beers."

We're half way through the first one when the door opens and floods the place with light. I glance over and recognize the silhouette in the doorway, cowboy hat square on his head.

"Sheriff Petersen," I call out. "How about that beer I owe you?"

He wanders on in, hangs his hat on a rack near the door, then climbs up to the bar next to Pax and extends his hand. "I'm Mark Petersen."

Pax shakes with him. "Sheriff, I believe Mike called you."

"He called me right." Then he eyes me. "You got a minute to step outside. I need a serious chat with you?"

Chapter Twenty

I stand, and motion to the sheriff, "How about we take that table over on the other side of the pool table?"

"Suits me," he says, then yells at Al. "Coffee please, Al," and heads over while Pax eyes us both curiously.

We sit across from each other but he waits for Al to put his coffee in front of him, and leave, before he begins. "You put Harley to work for you—"

"Harley? My bike?"

"Hunter's real name is Harley. And Al tells me you've been spying on this ARA bunch. That doesn't sound like fly fishing to me."

I have to laugh. "No, sir, not fishing for fish. I'm fishing for a missing person. Her folks hired me to find her, and bring her home if she's willing to come."

His jaw hardens. "I ought to throw you in the can for bullshitting."

"Bullshitting is no crime."

"It is if I say it is. I want you to stay away from that place, until I tell you otherwise."

"Because?"

"Because it ain't any of your business, that's what because it is."

"You've got some kind of op going on."

"I've had an interest in those crazies for a long time, but this thing over in Hamilton has picked up the steam."

"So," I say, a little coyly, "you think these were the guys who hit that fur farm and killed that kid?"

"Ravalli County Sheriff has his suspicions. There are three other groups in Montana who are animal nuts, and capable of being that crazy, but I'd put ARA right on top the list. So do me a big favor and stay out of the way. There's more to this than you know, or that I can tell you."

I stare out the window for a moment, then turn back to him. "Sheriff, you proved yourself to be a good ol' boy the other night when you didn't throw us all in the tank, so I'm gonna throw in with you. You give me a week and I'll hand you these guys...at least the bad part of these guys...on a platter with enough evidence to put them away for a good long while."

It's his turn to study me for a moment. "I'm making no deal with you, Reardon, as you're not a lawman...but I will tell you we don't have a case yet. In fact nowhere near a case yet. It'll be longer than a week before we do unless something untoward happens." He stares out the window for a moment, then turns back to me. "I know some of your background...some bad, more good. But you be real careful who you might be shooting at, even in self-defense. I'd hate to have you take down one of the good guys and have to go away to Deer Lodge for an extended visit...like life."

I eye him for a moment, then ask, "You've got a undercover guy in there, don't you?"

"Just be real careful. I gotta go...by the way, what's this guy, Pax...what's his last name?"

"Weatherwax, and run him all you want. He's Mr. Clean."

"You keep yourself clean."

"Yes, sir," I say as he heads for the hat rack.

Then he turns to Pax. "Hey, Weatherwax, keep your dog on a leash."

"I don't have a do—" Pax begins, then gets it. "He isn't mine, Sheriff, but you're right, he's the original junkyard dog. Nice meeting you."

"And I hope it stays nice," Petersen says as he settles the Stetson on his head, then pushes out the door.

We sip our way through two more Moose Drools as we split two games of eight ball, and just as it's getting good and dark outside, my phone vibrates.

"They're on their way back. They just passed Georgetown Lake and unless they stop in Phillipsburg will be there in thirty minutes."

"Good work, Hunter. Stop at the Vet's hall. I'm buying and you can fill us in."

"Us? Your buddy get in?"

"He did. See you in thirty…unless they stop again."

We get through one more beer and Pax has me down by two balls and him shooting for the eight. The two old cowboys who were in the bar the first day I walked in are at the bar, otherwise the place is empty.

This time when the door swings wide, it's the dim bar light spilling out, not sunshine spilling in, but the view is just fine. Inga Sorrensen wanders in, this time in those tight Lycra pants, high heels, and a gold blouse that shows enough nipple outline to make my mouth water. She spots me immediately and heads over. "You buying there, fast Eddy?"

I'd forgotten to tell Pax about the fact I'd tangled tongues with a beautiful blond while planting my bugs, and was well on my way to planting my caterpillar…or maybe I didn't want to put him onto the fact there was a beautiful blond.

"Wild Turkey, I presume?" I ask.

Pax is eyeballing her from blond hair, slightly spiked tonight, to high heels, and immediately extends a hand. "Hi, I'm Pax, and you're?"

"I'm thirsty, Paxman. Hasn't your buddy told you about me?" She gives me a dubious look.

"Not a word, the stingy bastard. But I'm all ears and have lots of time for you to tell me about you."

"Looks like you're in the middle of a game."

"I concede. Sometimes you gotta lose a little to win big," he says, and escorts her to the same table the sheriff and I had exited.

I come back from the bar with two more beers and a double Wild Turkey neat. And Pax and the blond are already eye-to-eye as if they've been sweethearts for the last ten years.

I barely get seated when she advises. "I think they're coming back here on the way to the camp. I'd suggest you pick 'em up and lay 'em down getting out of here."

"Not likely," I say, and she smiles a little sadly, and shakes her head as if I'd lost my mind. So she returns her attention to Pax.

And I'm glad it's Pax, locking eyes with her, as the door again pushes open and is filled with a very big, very well-muscled Arne Rostov. He's got on a Gold's Gym tee shirt that's about to split at the seams, golden chest hair spouting over the neck rim, and Levis tight enough to count the hairs on his balls. His gaze snaps to where the three of us are tabled up, and he strides our way in Army issue combat boots, his whole crew in tandem. Before he even speaks, thirty ARA members have crowded into the bar behind.

Hell, only twenty-five of them are male, and only a half-dozen look to be bad-ass ex-Military. Hardly any problem at all—of course half or more of them are most likely carrying. It's a good thing Pax and I both still hold our pool cues and have a wall at our back. Of course, we, too, each have a Glock in the small of our backs, hidden under un-tucked shirts.

Rostov's eyes remind me of a cougar's. He glowers at me and I get the feeling when he looks at a woman it's as if he's already brutally raping her, and when at a man he's already castrating him if he seems the least of a threat, and if not, he's eviscerating him and has his heart in his hand and is ripping chunks out of it with his teeth while making the guttural sounds of a feeding carnivore. How can he appear as if there's blood dripping from the corners of his mouth when all that's really there is a smirk?

I can feel the muscles beginning to bunch in my thighs, hips, and shoulders.

Jane Jasper Remington is among only five women in the group, but she's staring at me...and I get the impression, a little wistfully. That's a new one. Maybe her attitude is changing?

Inga stands and, wisely, moves away from us toward the bar. She's carrying her drink. She glances back and then over at Rostov. I sense there's a chill rattling her backbone. She takes a stool, downs three or four fingers of booze, and orders another Wild Turkey as if the place was not just about to explode.

Rostov moves over by her, says something under his breath, and she shakes her head rather adamantly. Then he moves our way, fists clinched at his side. Bad body language, under the circumstance. Both Pax and I rise, and I casually put a foot up on the chair. But now my every muscle is taut and casual moves are a total sham.

He stops over two arm lengths away and looks us both up and down, a sneer curling one side of his lip.

I'm not surprised when the big Indian, Charley Many Dogs, moves up an arm's length behind Rostov, then is joined by Hutchins, the mountain climber, and by spike-hair scraggily-bearded John Sainz, nickname Saint, who I suspect might not be as bad a dude as the other three, as I think he has pure motivation...a true love of animals. But who knows?

There are still balls on the pool table, so I return Rostov's sneer. "If you guys wanna play, put your quarter up. You can have winners."

There are times in life when discretion is by far the better part of valor...and as a very large, very well cut, Arne Rostov—former Army Ranger who looks to have about two percent body fat—stands glaring at Pax and me with two dozen compatriots backing him up, this seems among the top of the list of times.

Chapter Twenty One

Before he can speak, tattooed Maggie McFadden sidles up behind him and barks over his shoulder. "That's the prick was giving us a bad time at the Sunshine Station."

Rostov cocks an ear toward her, but doesn't take his eyes off me. Then the white haired guy—Pasternak I think—who was guarding the gate when we were there walks in the door. Rostov, being the good boss he certainly must be—not—must have sent a relief to the gate guard who wasn't able to join them for supper.

Whitey is Pasternak, nickname Patsy. He strides straight over and he too adds to the problem. "That's him, chief. That's the prick I saw going up the hill behind your house. I think he was after your woman."

Rostov yells across the bar, addressing Inga's back. "That true, Sorrensen? This guy come calling like a cur in heat? Some kind of dirty butt lickin' dog...."

She glances over her shoulder, then faces the back bar again. "I met him with Maggie down at the Sunshine. This is the first time I've seen him since. They offered to buy me a drink, but I shined them on...isn't that right, Al?"

Al is behind the bar, a glass and towel in one hand, the phone in the other. She merely smiles, obviously more

113

interested in staying out of the argument, and hopefully calling the cops.

"That ain't our game," Rostov says, motioning with his chin at the pool table, his scarred face red around an ugly eyebrow scar under his dirty blond hair. He's square jawed, a Nordic type with ice blue eyes, and women probably find him attractive. If they can get by the heinous glare.

He continues. "Kicking ass is our game. Were you trespassing on ARA property?"

White-hair Pasternak has been staring at Pax, and then he adds fuel to the fire. "And that fucker is the one what come to the gate saying he was lost, about the time the ugly one was dickin' around your cabin."

I laugh. "Did the same lightning bolt that turned your hair white cook your sorry brain?"

Rostov starts to say something to Pax, and has taken his eyes off me, so I take the opportunity to bring the stubby end of the pool cue up from the floor and plant it deep into his crotch like I'm going to knock his balls out of the park. He makes a sound like he's choking up a pine cone, falls back into the arms of the big Indian, and Pasternak and Sainz stand with jaws dropped. The evil glaring eyes are now round as golf balls. But the bigger and uglier of the three, Hutchins, charges me, which gives Pax the opportunity to smash his nose with the blunt end of his pool cue. Blood gushes as he goes to his back, coughing, choking, and rolling back and forth in pain while trying to hold his supply of blood in his smashed nose.

Rostov has both hands on his crotch and he sinks to his knees. The Indian steps forward and takes a wild swing at me with a ham sized fist and I feel the whish of air go by my ear, but he misses clean, then merely watches me as I back out of his reach. His nose is still swollen from his last visit to the Vet's Hall and maybe he has second thoughts about taking another whack.

Pax and I head for the door with two dozen ARA members between it and us, swinging our pool cues as if we were thrashing weeds or going for a fast ball, and they scramble back as the whishing sound like a big league bat warns of a broken bone.

Then we're out into the night air, and I'm very, very surprised that we exit clean. We pass Hunter who's on his way in, and he looks a little confused. I yell at him, "Take a hike. The shit hit the fan in there. See you back at the barn."

In seconds Pax is in the van and I've fired up the Iron, and we peel out. I glance over my shoulder to see that Jane Jasper Remington has followed me out of the saloon. That could be a very good thing.

God is good, particularly if He's convinced her I'm one of the good guys.

We head straight back up the road to Hunter's cabin, which could be a mistake. There's only a couple of two-tracks as escape routes as the road plays out a few miles into the canyon, and you'd have to know the country to find them. Pax has brought a goose-down sleeping bag with him, and mine is always in the van. As soon as we get there we park the vehicles, hook a water hose up to the sink supply and an electrical cord to the van and leave a light on inside. The last place we want to be is cornered in an enclosed van with the possibility of two dozen shooters headed our way, but the fact is I want it to lure them in. We move up the hillside behind the cabin, Pax with the 7.62 SASS and me with a Mossberg combat shotgun and a box of double ought—no plug means five in the magazine and one in the chamber. And both of us have our Glocks with a couple of spare magazines. I have night vision goggles, and Pax a night vision scope.

Now we climb a hundred feet up the mountain and find a spot where we can see them far better than they can see us…and wait.

When they don't show up in an hour, we decide to unroll the bags and take turns standing two hour watches. The sun lights the high mountains before we decide the excitement is over for a while and, each taking a different route to recon the neighborhood, head back down to the van and cabin. Hunter's Jeep has not shown up and there are no lights in his cabin, which makes me wonder if he didn't go home with Al. Then as Pax and I are in a couple of folding chairs by the campfire having coffee, my phone vibrates. I note it's just before seven.

We'd been enjoying the fact we escaped unscathed from the Vet's Hall, and the fact the blood spilled was the other guys.

"Yo," I answer after noting it's an unknown caller.

"Mike, it's Al."

"What's up? Is Hunter with you?"

"Yes, unfortunately we're both in the Phillipsburg hospital and he's in very bad shape…critical, the doc says."

"What happened?"

Chapter Twenty Two

Al sobs for a moment before she continues. "He came in the Vet's Hall right after you and that Pax guy fought your way out, and those assholes from ARA ganged up on him. They would have killed him if the cops hadn't showed. Three of them are in the Phillipsburg jail—"

"Are you okay?"

"They didn't touch me. The boss guy dragged that blond girl out with him, so I don't know about her."

"Damn it, I saw Hunter outside and told him to haul ass. Is Rostov in the can?"

"The asshole...the boss guy...no, he hauled ass out the back. The big Indian, the guy they call Saint, and one they call Hutch. Hutchins, I think it is."

"I'm on my way."

"Good. Hunter asked about you. They got him pretty doped up. Doc says they're probably going to have to take out his spleen at the least. He's pretty busted up."

"You need anything?"

"Just some moral support."

There's nothing the two of us can do, so I leave Pax with the Harley and lead him to the cut-off where the forest service road goes above the camp. He has my good binocs and a pair of receivers to pick up the audio from both the bugs I planted, and a recording device. Both bugs have their own thirty two gig chips, in addition to the transmitter, but you have to physically recover them to get the recordings.

The Granite County Medical Center is more than you might expect from a county with only a little over four thousand population. It's a solid looking brick building with variegated colors and a flat roof. As I wheel into the parking lot, a helicopter is lifting off a pad in the rear, and a half dozen people are standing by a gurney, watching it go. One of them is without the typical hospital white coat or candy stripes.

As I hustle that way, Al turns and sees me coming, and jogs down and throws her arms around me, burying her face in my chest, and sobbing.

I wait a respectful few seconds, then ask, "That was Hunter in the chopper? Where are they taking him?"

"Missoula, to St. Patrick's."

"So, what's happening?"

"He got worse. Renal failure the doc said. They wouldn't let me fly with him so I'm driving over."

"Anything I can do…buy your breakfast, or what?"

"No, I've got to go. It's an hour over there and they'll have him in surgery or something by the time I get there. Can you come?"

"I can, but I think Hunter would prefer me taking care of business here. If they give you any trouble with his insurance or—"

"He ain't got no insurance since he got laid off at the lumber company."

"Call me if you need help."

"You going after those ARA guys?"

"You're better off not knowing."

118

"You have Hunter's cell number...I called you from his cell. I still have it with me."

"I do."

She eyes me carefully for a second, then says, very seriously, "Fuck those guys up if you can. Eye for eye and all that stuff."

I merely smile, and she heads for a little Honda parked nearby.

As I'm climbing up into the van, my phone vibrates. Pax never bothers with hello. "You ain't gonna believe this one, pard."

"Let me be the judge."

"They're planning to hit the bug hotel."

"Rocky Mountain Lab? I was afraid of that."

"One and the same. They've got an inside man...or in this case a woman as they said 'she'. The lady has worked herself up to being a lab tech if I heard right. The sound could have been better."

"When?"

"I didn't get a time or a day, but I get the impression they've moved up the schedule because of the kid getting killed. They think the heat is on."

I fire up the van and use the hands-free as I pull out of the parking lot. "How's your buddy doing?" Pax asks.

"Not good, they had a chopper haul him to a bigger hospital in Missoula."

"What's the plan?"

"You hang tight and keep an eye on things. I'll call you when I hit Maxville."

"Guess what else?"

"Enough with the guessing games."

"Okay, grumpy. It seems the blond bombshell, little Miss Remington, and some other gal they called Susie are

119

being held against their will...locked in a cabin with a guard. They took a little umbrage when they learned that Rostov and this guy Hutchins cut the kid's throat...it seems the kid was able to pull Rostov's mask off and got a good look at him. It was his death warrant."

"That's good news...that Miss Jane Jasper wants to get the hell out of Dodge."

"And even more interesting...and I won't make you guess...it ain't the ferrets and monkeys they want to free from Rocky Mountain Lab."

"So?"

"So they plan to snatch some little tiny creatures...bad bugs...and hold the whole country for ransom. The only term I recognized was Anthrax. They have a plane chartered, which they plan to commandeer when they board, and go somewhere where they can blackmail the whole friggin' U. S. of A."

"Ambitious boys."

"Eager, yes...eager to be dead boys, if I have my way."

"I'll be there soon."

But I don't get out of the parking lot, as Sheriff Mark Petersen swings in front of me, his red light glowing, and slides to a stop. He climbs out of the car and I notice he snaps the strap on his semi-auto free as he walks over to the driver's side window.

"Step out, Reardon."

I shrug, and comply.

"Hands on the vehicle, feet back," he commands, then adds. "You know the drill."

He relieves me of the Glock, runs his hands up and down my legs to make sure I don't have another hide-out, then steps back. "Okay, relax."

"What's up?" I ask.

He stands, arms folded, jaw clinched. "Word is you started that mess down at the Vets Hall."

"I was there, I threw one blow, then we got the hell out of there. We weren't around when the chicken shits ganged up on poor Hunter."

"Maybe you should have been."

"I ran into him on the way out and told him to get the hell out of there."

"His lady was inside. You should have known—"

"You're right, I should have, and I'm royally pissed at myself."

"The three boys I have locked up say you started the whole thing."

"Sheriff, look at me. One old country boy and his half crippled buddy! We'd start a battle with two dozen ugly old boys...half of whom have done hard time?" Pax would be pissed if he knew I called him a half-cripple, so I won't relate that part of the story. But it did make it better.

"Where are you headed?"

"Maxville."

"Stop at the Vets Hall and we'll talk more. I've got to go to Drummond, so it's on my way."

"You got it. Can I have my weapon back?"

"After we talk."

I shrug, and head out ahead of him. Hell, I've got a half dozen more, most larger, in the Van.

Chapter Twenty Three

As we get close I call Pax and tell him where we're headed, and he says he'll join up.

There's a big ol' beer barrel size boy behind the bar, filling in, I guess, for Al. He nods when I walk in, and frowns when I order a coffee, just as the sheriff follows and does the same.

"I'll have to brew it," he mumbles, as the sheriff and I cross the room and take 'our' table.

"We've gotta quit meeting like this," I say. "People will talk."

"Maybe down in Las Vegas where you're from. People up here know better."

"So, how's the investigation coming?"

He shrugs. "You first."

"Well, you got half the really bad boys locked up and out of the way, and I hear my lady wants out and they won't let her go, so I have an excuse."

"You want me to go in and poke around? To be truthful, I got no just cause without somebody filing a complaint, and I'd rather wait just a couple of days."

I shake my head. "No, sir. I don't want them doing something stupid to the girl. I have reason to believe she may know some things you'd like to know, so let's keep her alive. Besides, she's a payday for me."

He leans back in his chair and again folds his arms and furrows his brow. "So, this is no more than a payday for you?"

"Sheriff, a young woman is in way over her head. And the blond, Inga, seems to want to get the hell out of there as well. And to tell the truth, I think she's a pretty nice lady and she, too, may have gotten herself into something she didn't expect. I don't much like what I see up there, so give me a chance to maybe do some things you can't do…you know, bail enforcement badge and all."

He leans forward, lots more interested. "So, does one of those guys have a warrant out?"

I smile. "Hell, you're the sheriff. You'd know better than I."

"That's probably more bullshit, but I'll take it at face value. I'm gonna tell you something you probably shouldn't know."

Now it's my turn to lean forward. "Go for it."

"You don't have to be quite so careful if you have to return fire."

"So, one of the three guys you have locked up is your inside man."

"I didn't say that. It's your turn to take it at face value."

"And I will." And as I finish the statement, the door is shoved open and Pax walks in. He hesitates, seeing whom I'm sitting with, but I wave him over.

"Sheriff," he says, extending his hand.

Petersen shakes but doesn't bother standing. "Join us," he says, and Pax pulls up a chair, just as the big bartender wanders over and places mugs in front of the two of us, then looks at Pax. "I guess you want a cup of coffee?"

"Pepsi," Pax says.

"Coke," the bartender replies.

"That'll do," Pax says, and the bartender wanders away.

"Anything new up the canyon?" I ask Pax.

"Lot of activity," he replies.

"You guys been eyeballing the ARA camp?" the Sheriff asks.

Pax hesitates, so I answer. "We have. Recon, we'd call it in the Corps. But yes, we've had eyes on it for a couple of days. Legal, from up the mountain."

"And?"

"Nothing exciting," I lie, as I don't want him charging in and risking my payday, and even more so I want to end this threat my way…not the law's way.

The sheriff digs in his wallet and hands me his card. "That's got my cell number. You boys need us, you just yell."

"Yes, sir," I say and rise as he does. He touches the rim of his hatband, and heads for the door. I add his number to my cell, then yell after him, "Hey, Sheriff, my sidearm."

He nods, and waves me to follow, which I do, and he hands it over from under his front seat. I shove it into my belt at the small of my back, under my shirt as I return to our table.

The bartender heads over and flops a ticket on the table. Where else could you get three cups of coffee for a buck fifty?

I repeat the question to Pax, now that the sheriff has exited. "Now that the man is gone, what's new up the canyon?"

"Lot of activity. I think they may be moving out."

"The hell you say. I think we better be moving in and spring the ladies."

"There's only one cabin with a guard outside the door. It's pretty obvious where they got the ladies holed up."

"So, let's go get them."

"I learned a few more things while I was laying on my butt up on the mountain. Thanks to Safari and my trusty iPhone."

"Are we gonna play Jeopardy again, or are you gonna tell me."

"Anthrax is, of course, among the many bad bugs living at the Rocky Mountain Lab. Do you remember a dozen or more years ago, an Army scientist was involved in the murder of a magazine editor…using Anthrax?"

I shrug. "I don't remember."

"Well, he was. He committed suicide so he was never prosecuted. Four others died and over a dozen got sick as hell…and that was from just a few spores. I called Sol back at the office and he did a search of Rostov's computer and turned up lots of web searches for Anthrax and infectious diseases. We gotta stop these pricks before lots of innocent folks die. You sure we shouldn't just give Homeland Security a call?"

"We can move lots faster. When it comes down to the nut cuttin', I'll call security over at Rocky Mountain Lab and give them a heads up."

"Okay, so long as we stay way ahead of them." He toasts me with his coffee cup, and we head out and back to Hunter's cabin to make some plans for the evening.

Kick ass plans.

Chapter Twenty Four

Twice these ARA assholes have made me ashamed of myself, and I don't take that lightly. They killed a kid while I watched, even if I didn't know it was happening. They beat the double dogshit out of a new friend while I hightailed it up the road, now it seems like I ran with my tail between my legs. I'm heartsick over both, and I don't like being heartsick.

There's nothing like a good dose of revenge to cure heartsickness.

Our first piece of business is to get the ladies out of harm's way. Then it's to stop whatever these a-holes have planned.

Pax will take the Harley up to our overlook, with the 7.62 SASS and its night vision scope. I'll park the van out of sight in the trees, and out of sight of the front gate, as I'll need to transport at least three of the girls if I can successfully spring them from where they're being held in the cabin...hopefully they're still there. A guard being posted there will verify the fact. I'll go in on foot and try to take out the guard with a sap without waking the place. Pax will cover my intrusion and, I hope, my successful exit from the ARA compound.

We'll have our cell phones but will use our handheld Motorolas with ear buds for primary. I'm going in with my Glock, three extra sixteen shot clips, and my Mossberg combat shotgun with the first two of six rounds being beanbag non-lethal, the next four double ought buck, and a bandolier with another dozen. The Mossberg has a light mounted on the rails near the muzzle, but no laser sight. If you can't hit something with double ought, you should go into selling shoes or running a hot dog stand.

We'll rest up until midnight then hit the place.

"When's moonrise?" I ask Pax and he checks his laptop.

"We're golden. Not until four thirty AM."

"Cool."

Just as we decide to try and grab some zees, my phone vibrates and I see the caller is the sheriff. "Yes, sir," I answer.

"The Justice of the Peace put a hundred grand bail each on those three ARA assholes...really high for this part of the world...but they made bail via a bondsman in Helena, Max Isenberg, and I had to cut them loose a couple of hours ago. Max told me Rostov laid out thirty grand cash like it was chump change. Thought you'd like to know."

"Thanks for the heads up."

"My pleasure. Anything new up there?"

"No, sir," I lie. "We're about to call it a night."

"Sleep light. These guys have a hard-on for you two."

"Will do, Sheriff. Thanks again."

"I'm going ahead and swearing out a warrant on this Rostov guy for his participation in that fiasco at the Vet's Hall, and plan to go into the ARA compound in the morning...so I'd suggest you guys steer clear of the place."

"What's up?" Pax asks as I hang up.

"The big Indian and the other two are out of the hoosegow, and Petersen and his troops are hitting the ARA compound with a warrant for Rostov early in the morning. So it's propitious that we go in tonight."

"Let's get some rest," Pax says, setting the alarm on his iPhone for midnight.

As I suspected, I'm unable to sleep, but I do get three hours of relaxation before his phone dings a few times. Pax, who can sleep through an air raid, wakes and stretches.

I have a cap for the headlight on the Harley that dims the light to a small spot and only illuminates the road for a dozen feet. Pax will put it to use well before he gets where there's any possibility of his being seen from the camp. I'll roll up the road to the compound using only my parking lights and will kill them well before I could possibly be seen.

I get to where I want to back the van into a copse of lodgepole pine without running into an ARA vehicle coming or going, and just as I'm comfortable where it's positioned—as I have yet to get my radio ear bud in place—my cell phone vibrates. It's Pax.

"This is all wrong," he says.

"What?"

"There's only one pickup down there. There's no guard on the cabin and a guy moving around, and it looks like he's pouring something out of a five gallon gas can."

"You think he's torching the place?"

"Looks like it to me."

"I'm going in, balls to the wall."

"I'm set up. Hoora!"

I fire up the van and peel out. It's only another three hundred yards to the gate, but I'm going sixty when I smash through the wrought iron and see it flying ahead of me.

Caught like a deer in the headlights is the white haired guy, Pasternak, with a red plastic five gallon gas can in hand. He's standing in front of the main building. He drops the gas can, throws a match to the ground at his back, and starts to run as I slide to a stop and jump out with Mossberg in hand. The front of the building goes up with a whoosh that says there's been lots of gasoline poured.

I'm wishing I had my double ought's in place, but then again we might want to question the asshole, just in case he's the only one left in the compound. I lay down on him and bust him in the small of the back from less than thirty yards, and he flies forward like he's been blindsided by a three hundred pound Raider's linebacker. As quickly as I can get beside him, I kick him hard in the ribs and roll him over.

"What's going on?" I command, but he's breathless for a second, then manages to mumble.

"Fuck you."

But he looks very frightened, and keeps glancing at the building . The whole front is already involved in flame. Then it dawns on me: The women!

I haul ass for the same side door I'd gone in to plant the bug, and this time find it locked. But it doesn't stand up against the second beanbag from only two feet. I have to duck as I charge into the big room as the smoke level is lowering fast, already down to four feet or so. And it's dark as hell, so I switch on the light on the muzzle of the Mossberg and pan it around.

Three bodies are in the middle of the room.

Am I too late?

Chapter Twenty Five

I crab across to the first one, who I may have seen when they all crowded into the Vet's Hall. She's a short fuzzy haired redhead. I put a finger on her carotid in her neck and get a pulse, but she's out cold. I hope the other two are merely unconscious as well.

I have to set the Mossberg aside, but do so, and drag her to the door and twenty feet outside. I'd drag her farther, but it was already getting hot in the middle of the big room, and I run like hell to get the second one, and realize it's the tall blond, Inga.

Selfishly, I'm thinking I should have dragged Jane Jasper Remington, my payday, out first, but I take them as they come. Inga is bigger and more of a load than the redhead, but I get her out and on the ground, then charge back in. Jane Jasper is shorter, but equally as heavy as Inga. My eyes are burning badly with the smoke, and I'm trying to hold my breath. I decide it'll take too long to drag her, so I get her up and do a fireman's carry and charge for where I can no longer see the door, but think I know where it is. I miss, and bounce off the log wall and we both go down hard. But as fate will have it, from flat on my back I can see the opening under the last foot of smoke free space, and roll, grab her under the arms, and heaving and huffing am outside. I can't see a damn thing as my eyes are burning and tearing, but it's easy to know where to go—away from the heat, which is beginning to sear my hair, eyebrows and lashes.

Even though unconscious, Jane Jasper is coughing, and I follow suit, trying to clear my lungs.

I do get some vision back, and sit up to a very unpleasant sight. The white haired guy is stumbling my way, one hand behind him, rubbing his back. Passing a tool rack lined with shovels, hoes and rake—and a few hand tools—he grabs one up. As he nears I suddenly realize he has a machete, and he looks as if he intends to fillet or behead me.

And I've left the Mossberg inside, now a raging inferno.

However, he only gets to about ten feet away, when his head explodes like a melon and his evil grin turns to an open mouth full of blood. He slams to his side on the ground, soaking it in brain and blood.

Thank you, Mr. Weatherwax.

I drop to my back and cough for a while, not bothering to answer my vibrating iPhone, until I realize that even where we are, the heat is getting too intense. I have to act, and again go to work, dragging the ladies, one at a time, until we are each fifty feet, then dragging them again until a hundred feet from the now totally involved structure.

It's all I can do to get my legs under me, but I do so and get to the van and get it over to the women. As I'm loading the first one, I see the single light of a motorcycle careening into the compound. Happily, it's Pax.

"You didn't answer your phone, dickhead!" he yells at me as he leaps off the bike and lends a hand loading the ladies.

"Sorry, dingus, I was a little busy. Good shot, by the way. Did you pick up your brass?"

"Didn't throw the bolt. You don't have to if the first shot counts. But, thanks. No hill for a stepper."

In moments we're hauling ass out of there, as I hope we'll beat the incoming fire trucks and cop cars, which I'm sure are on their way. Then I realize the compound can't be seen from the highway. Unless someone is camped high in the mountains or flying overhead, the fire will go unseen, and probably undiscovered, until the sheriff makes his raid in the morning or it lights up the whole forest and half the state shows up to fight fire.

Luckily, the forest is very wet and there is over a hundred feet separating the burning building from other structures or trees. Still, I dig a throwaway phone out of the glove compartment of the van and make a 911 call and report the fire.

I'd hate, hate, hate to have the whole damn mountain go up in flames.

With Pax following me, we stop in the parking lot of the Vet's Hall and check on the women, who are still out cold.

It's not yet two AM, and the place is still open with a half dozen diehards' cars and pickups parked outside. One of the trucks is a crew cab, with room to hold all three ladies.

"Drugged, you think?" I ask Pax.

"Ruffies, I'll bet," he says, and again checks. "They all three have strong pulses."

"I hope it's ruffies...if so they'll be okay tomorrow. But we've got to get them some help in case it's something worse."

"I'll see who's in the bar," Pax says.

"No, I'll see who's in the bar, you get on your laptop and see where the ARA cars are headed."

"You're right. Go."

There are two couples playing pool, two more throwing darts, and the same two old cowboys I've seen before at the bar.

"Whose crew cab pickup is outside?" I yell loud enough to be heard over the juke box and Big and Rich wailing away.

One of the old cowboys looks over and eyes me up and down. "Who wants to know?" he asks.

"I've got some injured ladies outside who need a ride to the hospital."

"Injured how?" he asks, but he's on his feet and moving toward the door with his buddy close behind. Everyone in the place follows.

As soon as he sees the women stretched out in the van, he again gives me a look, only this one is hard and suspicious. "What the hell's going on here? Why don't you haul them to the hospital? How the hell do I know you two didn't do something to them?"

Chapter Twenty Six

I try to be patient, although I don't feel it. "I think they've been drugged." I reach in my back pocket and flip open my wallet, showing him my bail enforcement officer's badge, hoping he won't insist on a close look, as a couple of day's training, the sponsorship of a bondsman or other bail enforcement officer, and thirty-five bucks for the brass is all it takes. Then I add, "I'm going after the guys who did this."

Just about that time, two hundred yards away on Highway 1, a fire truck with a following sheriff's car passes, sirens and lights blaring.

So I add, "And they set some buildings on fire up the canyon."

"Get them in the pickup," he says with a hint of a southern drawl, and a couple of the other guys pitch in to help me transfer them. As soon as we do, one of the pool playing women offers to ride along, and climbs in and they're off to Phillipsburg. I turn to another of the ladies, "Call the hospital and tell them they're on their way. I'd guess it's ruffies, but don't know."

"What's a 'ruffies'?" she asks. Sometimes I forget I'm in the boondocks.

"Just tell them, please."

Then I get the bad news. Pax walks over. "They must have found your tracking devices. I'm getting nothing."

"They were getting suspicious. How about cell phones?" I ask.

"Negative. Nothing."

"Okay. Obviously they're onto the fact they're being watched and have stepped up their agenda. Where's the worst possible place they could be heading?" I ask, knowing the answer.

"The Rocky Mountain Lab," he says, and is dead on the money.

"I wonder how long they've been gone from the compound".

"Way less than an hour, possibly," Pax reasons. "If the guy was left behind to burn the place down, then they probably went out just before we went in."

"Okay," I say, and dig into my phone contacts and find Hunter's cell number. On the seventh or eighth ring, Al answers, sleepily.

"Hel...Hello," she says.

"Al, it's Mike Reardon. I need your help."

"I was asleep in the waiting room. My back's killing me."

"Then you can probably use getting up and moving around. These ARA guys are on the move. I need you to get out to Highway 93 just as it heads south out of town, and watch for them. They are in a half dozen of their cars and you can't miss them. Get out there and call me back if you see them."

"This is something you really need?" she asks, again yawning.

"You want me to get even with whoever busted Hunter up?"

"Yes," she says, this time adamantly. "He's still in Critical Care. They took out his spleen and had to put some pins in his leg, and he's in traction. He had a break in his wrist and has a cast there."

"At least he's alive. So go. I'm headed that way."

"Okay, I'll call if I see them," she says, and hangs up.

I'm about out of throwaway cell phones, and dig into the glove compartment and find one more. As we're hauling ass toward Missoula, Pax driving and the speedometer bouncing off a hundred when there are no headlights in sight, I dig for the number of the Rocky Mountain Lab. I get it, call, and, of course, get a recording. Having no other choice, I call the Ravalli County Sheriff's Office and a kid, who sounds about fifteen, answers. "Dispatch."

"I have reason to believe that someone will try and break into the Rocky Mountain Lab tonight."

"Your name and telephone number?" he asks.

"Doesn't matter. Can you patch me through to the sheriff?"

"Your name and telephone number?" he asks again.

"How about the officer on duty?"

"Look, how am I supposed to know if this is a crank call or not? We get lots of stuff about the—"

"Look, kid, patch me through to someone with a brain." It appears that was not a constructive response on my part.

"Name and phone number or I'm hanging up."

"Wait, wait. Can you give me the number of security at the Rocky Mountain Lab?"

He rolls off a telephone number as if it's taped to the wall over his desk and I make note of it, hang up, then realize it's the same number I'd dialed that got me a recording.

Fuck.

Then I realize that the little town of Hamilton has a police department, dig for their number on the web, and find it. This time it's a woman who answers. "Hamilton Police. No one's in the office. If this is an emergency please dial 911."

A bloody recording. So I do. "911. What's your emergency?"

"I need to have you patch me through to security at Rocky Mountain Lab."

"This is 911, sir. What's your name and your emergency."

"Please patch me through."

"Sir, this is not a secretarial service. This is the 911 emergency number. Your name and the nature of your emergency please."

"My name is John Miller and the nature of my emergency is I have information that some very bad people are going to try and break into the Rocky Mountain Lab."

"We have pickets there often, sir."

"I'm talking break in here."

"I'll let the officer on patrol in the area know."

"And their security?"

"He'll stop by."

"And Homeland Security?"

"He'll stop by the Lab."

So, I hang up and turn to Pax. We're in the middle of Missoula but making good time as there's no one on the road. "Step on it. It looks like it's up to us."

Chapter Twenty Seven

My phone vibrates as soon as I hang up from the 911 call and I see it's Hunter's cell phone calling.

"Al, what's up?" I answer.

"There are only two cars. That gray Jeep Rubicon and a white Dodge pickup with three guys in the front seat. It's a good thing they're in that fancy Jeep or I might not have noticed. I can't tell how many are in the Jeep."

"Only two vehicles? You sure the others aren't behind...stopped by a red light or something?"

"I can't see anyone else."

"Did they see you?"

"Nope. I'm in a parking lot a couple of hundred feet from Highway 93."

"Can you follow them without being seen?"

"I guess."

"We're maybe a mile behind. We'll catch up as soon as we get through town and take over for you."

"Good. I need to get back to the hospital."

We catch up to Hunter's Jeep by the second stoplight in the little town of Lolo, and pull up beside her. I yell over. "Thanks, Al, I owe you. Get back and take care of Hunter."

"Be careful," she yells back, and turns off into a parking lot to turn around. In less than a minute we're a hundred yards behind the white Dodge pickup and see the Rubicon up ahead, so we, too, turn off and let them get a few hundred yards in front of us. We're still a half hour to Hamilton, and it wouldn't do to be made by them...so we play it very casual. The van is easy to spot as it's pretty big and white. We have to be careful.

We have to swing to the curb and kill our lights shortly after we cross the river and enter Hamilton, as they are ahead of us only a block and a half, and are stopped at a light.

Oops, they split up, with the pickup going straight ahead and the Rubicon turning right onto main street, which is little more than two blocks of businesses, and where I had lunch during my visit here.

"What do you think?" I ask Pax.

"Jeep. That one is registered to Rostov and I'm sure he's driving."

"Jeep it is."

Pax gives them time to get a couple of blocks ahead, then makes the turn and follows. As we exit town going west, we cross the river again. I know the Bitterroot River is the west boundary of Rocky Mountain Lab property, so am a little surprised, until I see the Jeep's brake lights come on and the vehicle swerves across the oncoming lane and pulls up in front of a barbed wire fence. I have to use my binocs as soon as Pax again kills his lights, and see that one of them is out with a pair of bolt cutters and quickly snips the four strands away.

"You think we can follow?" I ask Pax. "It looks like lots of underbrush out there."

There's a fallow field for the first two hundred yards, an orchard of some kind to the west, but riparian brush and trees up ahead.

Pax is studying a Google Earth picture on his laptop, then glances up. "All we can do is give it a try. We can always flip a u-turn and head for the lab and give a heads up to security."

"Fuck that. These guys are up to no good, tried to cook the ladies after doping them, and would probably get off with a malicious mischief charge even if they got nailed. Better we solve the problem."

"It's equivalent to about six city blocks, maybe three quarters of a mile, until we're even with the back of the lab. They should be easy to track in the mud and sand."

"Yeah, but they can get across the river with that breather, and we can't if it's over a foot deep and I'll bet it's twice that."

"You're due for a bath anyway. It can't be more than a couple of hundred yards from the river to the security fence, so we'll hoof it."

"Swim it and hoof it, probably."

"Fuck it, it ain't that cold out."

I make my way to the back of the van and dig out an S&W15 and a couple of extra clips. We suit up, adding vests, and I get my little 22 Mag five shot and strap it on in its ankle holster. And we take off, into the lion's den.

Pax is driving with just his parking lights. He's having to weave in and out of hundred-year-old cottonwoods, a few aspens or elms, and lots of river willow which is ten foot high and thick in spots…a good thing, as it occludes the view of us following. A bad thing as we might drive right up on them without realizing they've stopped.

We've got good starlight, and I realize it must be nearing dawn as the moon is over the mountains to the east and was due to rise at 4:30. Now it's a benefit to us as it's casting moon shadows. Pax is able to kill even the parking lights.

"We've got to be getting close," Pax says as he's watching the odometer.

"Let's move up on foot. I'd hate to drive up on them."

So we unload. As usual, Pax leaves the keys under the front seat in case one of us gets back without the other. We're still dressed dark, and Pax still has his night vision scope on the SASS and I have my night vision binocs, so, hopefully, we have some advantage.

Trying to stay at least twenty yards apart so as not to both be taken out with the same burst of automatic fire or spread of double ought buck, we stay low and move around the thick cottonwood trunks and through the willows.

After less than a hundred yards we come upon a flow of water, only ten yards across and barely ankle deep as we cross. It has to be a side channel, not nearly as large as the main river. The tracks of the jeep have charged right on across as if it's nothing, and it shouldn't be as the jeep has a breather at least five feet off the surface.

Then we're in thick brush again.

I freeze as the stop lights on the Jeep flare brightly, not thirty yards in front of me.

Chapter Twenty Eight

I hear someone shout "Don't slow down," and the Jeep charges into the main river. I can see the water flare to both sides in the moonlight.

To be truthful I'm hoping there's a ten foot deep hole out there in the forty yard wide river, but doubt it, as I'm sure they've reconnoitered this crossing, and they barely slow until they're climbing the bank on the far side.

As soon as they top the rise they're out of sight again. The crossing is little deeper than the side channel had been, and now I'm pissed we didn't come on with the van, it can't be another couple of hundred yards to the security fence, so it's probably just as well.

I top the rise on foot, not wet even up to my knees, and realize Pax is out of sight. With one leg slightly shorter than the other and lifts on one shoe, he may have had trouble crossing, but I won't mention it.

Pulling my handheld out, I give him a buzz, and get a buzz right back. I whisper, "Let's join up. Work your way up river and I'll sit tight."

"Roger," comes a whispered reply. "They've stopped about a hundred yards ahead."

I wait until I can make him out, easing out of the river willows only twenty yards from me, and move to join him.

"You okay?" I ask.

"When the fuck wasn't I okay," he snaps back.

"Sorry I asked. You flank them on the left, I'll do so on the right. If they try and cut or blow the fence, I'm ready to send them to hell."

"Righteous," he says, and we again split up. I find a log and get prone behind it, throw the safety on the S&M15, then pick up my night vision binocs and zero in or what's going on up ahead, and see two guys are unloading—thank God there's enough light to spot the targets in my scope if I'm convinced who they are and what they're doing via the night vision binocs. One of them carries what looks like a satchel charge. I lay down on him and begin to put pressure on the trigger, when an explosion rocks me and I recover to see flame and smoke billowing from somewhere in the front of the complex.

I guess the three guys in the pickup have been busy as well. I'll be pissed at myself if they've taken out the guard shack and a couple of guards along with it.

So I drop the guy with the satchel, stitching his back with a three shot burst from my hundred yard position. At almost the same time I hear the 7.62 roar off to my left. The second guy who'd exited the Jeep has hit the ground so hard I'm sure it's being slammed down from a centered head-shot. I get a glance at a reflection in the moonlight and think it's the spiked-hair guy whose spikes are now filled with bone, blood, and brains. No problem for Pax at a hundred yards. But it could be a very big problem for both of us if he's the undercover guy. He was one of the three in the Phillipsburg Jail, and I'm sure one of them was at least an informant, if not an agent or lawman.

The Jeep is slammed into reverse and is throwing mud out in front of it as it spins all fours coming back, its engine screaming.

Another 7.62 shot roars in the night and the rear tire on the driver's side flattens as if a balloon burst, then another shot, almost as fast as the bolt could be thrown, and the passenger side tire also explodes. The driver grinds the gears and then is slathering forward. Pax fires again and the driver's side front tire explodes and the Jeep careens to the left and slams into a downed cottonwood that's at least three feet in diameter. He's not climbing over that one.

I put a burst through the back window, and it explodes as if a satchel charge was set off behind it.

Silence.

Then the driver's door opens and two hands emerge as if the arms and body they're attached to are lying down in the seat. An attempt, it appears, at surrender.

I'm not interested in surrender, but I'm less interested in shooting down some son of a bitch who's trying to do so. I'm very disappointed when Arnold Rostov emerges from the Jeep with his hands on his head.

And I so wanted to blow the son of a bitch into hell.

In my best bounty hunter mode, I yell out as I get to my feet, "Feet back, hands on the vehicle, legs spread." And he does so as if he's done so a dozen times before.

Pax and I both move forward until we're a dozen feet from him, when a voice rings out behind us.

"Drop the weapons, and don't fucking twitch or you're both dead."

Pax and I glance over at each other, both of us thinking that what do we have to lose, when a high-

144

pitched female voice follows. "Please, please, do as they say."

We both still have Glocks in the small of our back, so both of us sigh and let the long arms fall to the ground. It sounds as if they have one of the young ARA women with them, and the last thing I want to do is spray a college age do-gooder coed with lead.

We turn slowly to see the big Indian, Charley Many Dogs, holding a handgun; Maggie McFadden has an evil grin and is holding a pump shotgun; and the badass Hutchins holds what looks to be an AR15 and he, too, is laughing.

Maggie stops her cackle long enough to chide us with a voice now two octaves lower than the girlish one she'd just used. "You dumb fucks thought I was one of those stupid young cock-sucking college girls, didn't you?"

"Doubt it, Maggie," I can't help but say. "You flew a broom here and they couldn't."

"Fuck you, Reardon."

"You got no chance of that, you crusty old rotten bitch."

Charley Many Dogs snaps at them. "You two go over and frisk them."

"Why keep them alive?" Hutchins asks.

"Hostages, until we get to the plane."

Hutchins shrugs, and growls at Maggie, "Come on."

But they only take two steps, as Many Dogs has holstered his weapon. He steps forward and with his massive ham sized hands reaches out and smashes their heads together. Maggie goes down flat on her face as if he'd hit her with a boulder and Hutchins sinks to his knees. Many Dogs smashes Hutchins across the side of the head with his heavy semi-auto hard enough that it sounds like a watermelon has been dropped from a second storey window.

Both Pax and I are going for the Glocks in the small of our backs, but Many Dogs is panning his weapon back and forth from one of us to the other and has his other hand extended, palm out.

"Don't draw those. I'm FBI. The sheriff put me wise to you guys or you'd be full of holes. An FBI team is on their way here from Missoula...but they're still thirty minutes out."

Pax and I glance at each other, both slightly astounded. Then we realize something we hadn't noticed. Then I say, "And you're the last one I figured...."

I yell at the Indian, "Damn it, Rostov is gone."

Chapter Twenty Nine

Many Dogs drags Hutchins and McFadden over to a twelve inch diameter cottonwood and puts the cuffs on them, her right wrist to his left, her left to his right, circling the tree.

"They got bears in this forest," I advise him.

"Hungry ones I hope," he says. "You have no idea what pricks these people are."

"Oh, yeah. They were gonna burn three of their members alive."

He stares at me a moment, then I can see his jaw harden. "They said they were leaving them tied up and would call someone to find them when this was over."

"They left them drugged up, unconscious, on the floor of the main building while that white haired prick spread gasoline and lit it up."

"And?" he asks, looking like he might be sick.

"And we got there in time."

"And you turned Pasternak over to the sheriff."

"Not exactly, but you don't want to know."

He shakes his big head slowly. "Yeah, what I don't know won't hurt you."

"Let's go after Rostov."

He gives the Jeep a frustrated glare. "You fucked up our ride."

"Our van is back aways, as is my Harley. We got rides."

I take off at a brisk walk.

"Good. We left two bikes parked a block from the lab in their confederates carport...Rostov's V-Tec and a smaller Yahama. I'm sure that's where Rostov is headed."

"Let's beat him there." I move it up to a fast jog.

Many Dogs yells behind me. "I doubt it. The son of a bitch is in real good shape. He runs five miles every morning up and down the canyon and bench presses four hundred."

I look back over my shoulder. "I'll take the Harley. You guys catch up in the van."

"Gray and pink house on Desta and South Fourth."

"Got it," and I go ahead and break into a run. Pax can jog five miles hardly working up a sweat, but a flat out run is hard on his short leg. However, I'm sure he can keep up with the three hundred pound plus FBI man. "Turn the ring up on your phone. Stay on your radio," I shout behind.

I don't bother with the ramp, but gun the bike out of the van, almost losing it in the soft sand. But I get control and am out of the field and on the road in less than a minute, and hit it hard on W. Main back into town. Then I realize I have no idea where 4th and Desta is, but the first cross street I come to is 9th, and they're going down. I mentally flip a coin and turn right on 4th, which takes me south and I think he said south 4th, and am a block from its end when I come to Desta.

It's beginning to be light, but I have to stop in the center of the intersection to try and make out which house is pink and gray, then spot it and a motorcycle in its carport. And it's a Yamaha. If the V-Tec was there, it's gone. Now, where the hell would he head to? The airport of course. They have a plane chartered. Then, before I can gun it, I feel my phone vibrate in my pocket.

"Yo," I answer.

It's Pax. "Any luck?"

"Nope, he's gone—."

"We're headed for the airport. Take Main Street east, it swerves north...watch for the signs."

"Got it." I retrace my route.

If a cop sees me hauling ass through town, running the town's only stoplight and breaking the speed limit by at least twice, he'll be after me. Which might not be all bad, as he can help out. I swing north and soon find a sign pointing east to the airport.

The van is waiting, idling at the parking lot entrance, when I roar up alongside and find Pax driving and Many Dogs in the passenger seat.

He yells over the noise of the bike, "The V-Tec is over there next to the building, but I don't see our guy."

"A plane?"

"A half dozen on the tarmac. No lights anywhere. You head north along the runway, we'll go south." And he peels out, so I comply. As soon as I get clear of the buildings I realize there's not a plane on my end of the runway, but turn the bike and head out so I can see its full length. And sure as hell, there are running lights on the far end, a half mile away, and they're headed my way. I notice a nearby windsock, facing away from me, so takeoff will start from Pax's end heading into the wind.

Then I spot the van. Pax has also rolled out onto the edge of the runway and I see his interior light come on. He must be exiting the van.

149

The plane's landing lights come on and it's roaring my way, then I see the muzzle flash of the SASS, and pray that it's our guy Rostov trying to escape in what appears to be a v-tail Bonanza, and not some doctor off on a jaunt. The crack of the 7.62 reaches me.

The plane is headed north, my way, nearing take-off speed…but suddenly a tire goes flat and it veers off the runway, crosses fifty feet of taxiway and tangles with one of the parked planes, wing on wing sparks flying, and spins. Then its tail hits another wing on a second plane and lights up the night with a flash and a gargantuan roar—the explosion of aviation fuel—as the Cessna it hit explodes in a ball of fire.

The Bonanza is blown over on its top, one wing ablaze, and I'm sure it'll blow all to hell in a heartbeat.

Chapter Thirty

But it doesn't blow and I doubt they can get out the door, as a Bonanza door is curved over the top of the fuselage and I know the full weight of the plane's on it. Then I see they've kicked the windscreen out and are coming out under the engine... two men on all fours. They hit the pavement and are up at a dead run. The taller and broader of the two, who I'm sure is Rostov, is already twenty feet in the lead, and rounds a building corner and is out of sight. The Bonanza goes up with a resounding explosion. The runner following Rostov is blown off his feet, but is managing to recover as I kick it into low gear.

There's no way I can get back before he's to his bike, but I spin the wheel, throwing gravel out behind and fishtailing as I give it the old college try.

Before I'm halfway, another plane, this time a twin, goes up with an explosion that damn near knocks me down and the heat sears my face...but I manage to get her back on track. Just as I reach the edge of the small terminal building, I see a taillight already two hundred yards ahead and disappearing into the growing light.

Then, far ahead, I see a big black vehicle slide sideways in a billow of dust, attempting to block the road. But Rostov doesn't slow, and before anyone can exit the vehicle, I see muzzle flashes then hear the reports of four shots coming from the rider, not from what now looks to be a Ford Expedition. Its windows are spider-webbed from Rostov's gunshots.

The front passenger side door opens as I close the distance and I slow just long enough to yell at a guy who's pulling his weapon. He has on a black vest and I can just make out FBI in gold letters.

I hold up a hand, palm extended, and shout "You guys okay?"

"You Reardon?" he asks, and I nod.

"We got a man down in the back. We're calling for a medevac."

"I'll get that prick." I glance over my shoulder to see my van, Pax driving, closing fast. But I don't have time to shoot the bull if I'm to get a shot at stopping Rostov, and gun it around the expedition just in time to see the big Honda three hundred plus yards ahead lay hard into a fast left hand turn.

Let's see, what is likely to be a hundred mile an hour plus chase and I didn't bother to grab a helmet? What the hell, you'd die anyway if you piled it up at a hundred plus, so you might as well die fast.

The wicked looking V-Tec is a faster bike than my Iron, but I think my Iron is way tougher, and as I'm cruising along behind Rostov I'm pleased to see he turns east onto the Skalkaho Highway, knowing that it becomes gravel and dirt after a few miles. The only thing better would be if he tried to lose me off road, as I've spent many days in the Nevada and California deserts, although they were on a Yahama dirt bike. Still, I think I can take him easy if he gets off road.

When we hit the dirt, I try and close the distance. It's full light and he can see me easily in his rear view as I close to within a hundred yards...and it's plain he does, as he kicks it in the ass and begins to pull away. The good news is when he hits eighty on the dirt, the curves are coming fast and furious, and there's no way he can get anywhere near top end under the conditions. The bad news again is he's kicking up dust and even some gravel, and it's gonna be tough to close on him.

I know that Pax and Charley Many Dogs are back behind us, kicking up even more dust than we are in the van.

We're riding into the rising sun, and as it's low over the mountains, it's blinding. With any luck he'll take a tree head on and solve my problem. Before long there's a creek on the north side of the road, and we're following it, with the road taking every turn it does.

The old adage of being able to tell a motorcycle dude because of the bugs in his teeth won't work on me, as it's dust and gravel peppering me every time I try and get close, and I don't have a helmet and visor and can't take the time to stop and put on my sunglasses. It's the shits.

We haul ass for over a dozen miles.

Then God smiles on me.

A fully loaded log truck rounds a curve, a wide turn and suddenly Rostov has a massive grill and the bulldog hood ornament of a Mack truck in front of him. He brakes hard, almost laying her down, then recovers and has to go on the inside of the huge truck. He shoots off into the brush, and I hope he's found a deep hole in the creek and his bike and he are underwater.

But I can't find out quite yet, as the truck driver has panic all over his mug and locks it up, and suddenly all I can see is a fully loaded log trailer trying to pass the tractor which is chattering my way with brakes locked.

Luckily I'm far enough that I can slide to a stop and manage to reach a standstill ten feet from his cab. He's an older guy, gray hair and beard, and his mouth is hanging open as he gasps for breath. He kills the engine, much to my dismay, and is fully blocking the narrow road.

I idle it down and shout. "Law officer. Chasing that guy. Can you ease it forward enough so I can get around?"

"Fuck you," he yells, "you guys are fucking nuts."

Chapter Thirty One

Again, my bail enforcement badge comes in handy and I dig my wallet out and flash it. "You're interfering with an officer in the line of duty. Ten years in the pen, pardner."

His face goes blank. I have no idea what I'm talking about, but it works and he cranks the engine back up and engages the gears and I have to fire it up and do a one eighty. As soon as I have three feet of clearance, I skinny around him and see where the V-Tec has cut a path through the brush and follow for twenty feet, bouncing over rocks and deadfall, to the edge of the stream. Unfortunately, there's no hole, in fact it's less than a foot deep and only twenty feet across, and I can see where he busted brush on the other side. Then I look up the hill and see there's a two-track road a hundred yards up the slope, twenty five yards above the creek, and there's a trail of dust disappearing into the heavy forest a quarter mile away.

I can't see Rostov and his bike, but I know where he's gone.

A two-track. Now the advantage should be mine.

It's time to make it end.

After a small hill climb I'm on the timber company road he's using, his tracks so easily followed he might as well have been trailing red paint. I bust out of a copse of lodgepole pine to see a fairly large drainage with the road fairly level in a horseshoe shape a few hundred yards across, and I see him kicking up dust a few hundred yards ahead of me on the road, but only a couple of hundred across the drainage as the crow flies. If I had the SASS I'd have a reasonable shot at him. Then he disappears into another deep dark forest of tall ponderosa, and I hit the throttle hard, leaning into the long slow turn until I, too, am nearing the huge stand of ponderosa.

I've passed a couple of drift fences, barbed wire, and there's one on the near side of the trees I'm rapidly closing on, with a speedometer saying sixty mph.

Too late I see that he's knocked the top strand of barbwire loose from a pull gate, and it's now an almost invisible garrote about neck high. I have to put on the binders, then lay it down in order to slide under the killer wire. And I do slide on the grass and dirt road, for at least sixty or seventy feet. Kicking free of the bike the last twenty.

I scramble to my feet in time to see him charge out of the trees only another thirty yards down the road, handgun spitting fire. I dive back to the ground and scramble away. The road is exploding all around me with plumes and I dive for the brush on the downhill side and roll and scramble, crabbing on all fours, into the trees and underbrush.

As soon as I feel I'm sufficiently out of his line of sight, I dig for the Glock at the small of my back…and it's not there. It must have pulled free as I slid down the road.

Fuck.

I get to my feet and run another fifty yards into the woods, downhill, then stop and, thank God, find the little five shot 22 mag in its ankle holster.

Let's see, I have five 22 mag shells against his sixteen shot 9 or 40mm, and he's probably got at least another magazine of sixteen…maybe two.

Then, to add injury to insult, I realize he's clipped me on the upper right arm, and I'm bleeding pretty good.

Time for another strategic retreat, so I run another fifty yards down the hill, dodging through two and three foot diameter ponderosa pines, with a carpet of thick ferns beneath.

I rip my flannel shirt off, then the tee shirt, and grab my five inch blade hunting knife from its belt scabbard and cut chunks from the tee shirt. The arm is creased, maybe a half inch deep, so I stuff it as best I can then wrap and tie strips from the tee shirt, binding the wound pretty well, having to use my teeth to secure one end. And then put the flannel back on.

"Hey, asshole," rings out from what I estimate is sixty or seventy yards up the hill.

And he thinks I'm dumb enough to answer?

Instead, I do the opposite of what he thinks a wounded man would do…and I'm sure he knows I'm hit as I must have left some blood trail.

I circle to the east, trying to get what advantage I can from the sun at my back and in his eyes. It's now ten or fifteen degrees above the horizon, so should offer some help as I go uphill, not the direction most wounded animals would take. Uphill, and away from the road and thick willows along the creek most men would head for.

"Asshole…," he yells again, stringing it out.

And I still don't answer.

Among the ponderosa are a few firs, some only a foot in diameter, and they have lots of low branches. I'm thinking of climbing one and getting out of his line of sight, with the hope he'll cross below me close enough that I can be assured of a head shot with the tiny 22 mag, but then I hear him breaking brush, only thirty or forty yards behind me.

No time to climb. He's almost on me.

Chapter Thirty Two

No time to climb, but there's a thirty yard wide clearing ahead, and I'll never get across it before he breaks out and sees me.

Think fast.

There's a fist sized boulder in reach, so I grab it up and aim as far to his right as I think I can heave, and do so, landing it thirty yards from where I think his location to be. The little boulder obliges and hits and rolls, making plenty of noise as it bounces along.

There's silence for a moment, then noise through the brush as he moves quickly toward where the boulder landed.

I've another decision, but decide that courage and the unexpected is the only thing that'll win this confrontation. As quietly as I can move, I head toward him and the spot I heaved the boulder.

I haven't moved twenty paces when he rises up out of the underbrush, facing ninety degrees away from me and twenty five or thirty yards down the hill toward the last sounds of the boulder.

Deciding it's now or never I cock the little 22 and lay down on his upper body...too far for a head shot, and fire.

He flinches, and spins my way, and I realize he has my Glock in one hand and a semi-auto in the other and I dive in the brush as he charges, firing one weapon then the other. Bark's flying in my face as I try and scramble away in the thick ferns.

The wop wop wop of a chopper is suddenly so loud I almost drop the little 22 and cover my ears, then realize he's affected the same way.

At a dead run, I charge out of the underbrush and catch him looking up at the chopper that's buzzing him.

As fast as I can fire, I put the next four shots at his head, the last one from only ten feet.

He goes over to his back, but firing from both hands as he does, and fire lights up my inner thigh, but as I close the next few feet I realize he won't be shooting any more. There's a nice little hole just over his right eye, just under a scar that might have once made the ladies think he's tough, rugged and handsome. The fact is…was…he was pretty damn tough and I'm glad I didn't have to outrun the muscle fuck through the trees for another mile or two.

He was tough, but thank God again he wasn't the world's best shot, particularly after taking a 22 mag to the side, passing through his bicep and into his chest, then one to the forehead.

I re-holster the 22 in my ankle grabber and limp up the mountain toward where I can hear the chopper winding down. As soon as I spot a couple of guys wearing FBI vests and carrying assault weapons with thirty shot banana clips, I clamp both hands on my head.

"On your knees, " one shouts as they near, and I'm happy to comply. I wish he'd said "on your back," so I could get some rest, but he didn't.

"The bad guy is down the hill," I motion with my head. "But he's history."

"You Reardon?" the other fibbi asks, and I nod.

"Yeah, I'm Reardon and I could use a first aid kit."

"Move back toward the chopper. Keep ten yards in front of me. You armed?"

"Ankle holster 22, but the weapon's empty. Where's Many Dogs?"

"He's coming along. He and your buddy are in a white van."

"Good, there's a cot in the back and I need to take a snooze. Something about a half-gallon of adrenaline coursing through your veins that tires you out."

"Soon as we shake you down and get a confirmation on your identity."

"Works for me," I say.

It's over a half hour before I'm bandaged up, shoulder and thigh. Had the thigh wound been a half inch deeper and clipped my femoral I'd probably have bled out and joined Rostov in Valhalla, or wherever I'm destined. But it seems it's not my time yet.

With Many Dogs driving, another agent in the van's passenger seat, and Pax in the back of the chopper with me and two agents carefully watching, we get a short ride back to St. Pat's hospital in Missoula. It'll take the van an hour or more to get where we'll be in ten or twelve minutes.

I can't convince them to let me bring my Harley Iron along, not that it would have fit. They assure me that their crime site guys and gals will take very good care of it.

The emergency room doc at St. Pat's does a great job in putting my leg back to almost one piece with three dozen well placed stitches and some staples, and stuffs the shoulder wound and assures me I can get a graft and you'll barely notice it. I assure him that among the hundred other scars on my beaten and battered old bod it makes little difference.

"You do look a little like you've survived train, plane, and rocket wrecks," he says, then adds, "you want a shot of morphine?"

"I don't imagine you got a shot of Jack Daniels?" I ask, and he shakes his head no.

"Then I'll wait."

The agent who's standing nearby gives me a tight smile. "You're not going to hit the bar for a while, sunshine. You're going to a holding cell until the boss gets in from Seattle, then you've got some explaining to do."

Pax, who's in a nearby chair, adds, "Yeah, Lucy, you got some 'splaining to do."

We're three days in and out of interview rooms in the Missoula Federal Building, the first two nights in holding cells, then a night in a Federal sponsored hotel. We did pass a couple of other rooms, one holding Hutchens and the other Maggie MacDonald. Many Dogs will be unhappy the bears didn't get indigestion trying to eat the pair.

The Doubletree Inn has a great restaurant, the Fin and Porter, and we waste no time denting the FBI expense account, until we're informed we're on our own. And we're also informed we'll be subpoenaed to testify in the trial of Hutchens and Maggie McDonald.

And I hate that fact, as the worst they'll get, even in Montana, is twenty five to life where they'll get three hots and a cot—unless they can prove Hutchins was on the knife that slit the kid's throat. I wish I could have pronounced sentence on them myself.

My Harley, at a contracted auto impoundment—which the feds also pay for—is in pretty good shape, considering. A little touch up on the paint and she'll be good as new. I suggest to Many Dogs that the FBI should at least let me have Rostov's V-Tec since we may have saved the nation from a terrible plague, but he is not impressed and informs me that what he owes me is a good old country ass whipping and if he sees me after he leaves the Bureau, I can rest assured that's just what I'll get.

I do not remind him that it was he, not me, sucking blood and kissing the floor the last time we met. Discretion is the better part of valor.

Now, to find Jane Jasper Remington and return her to daddy, and collect my million four.

Chapter Thirty Three

I discover from the desk that Jane Jasper Remington was released from the Phillipburg Medical Center ten hours after she arrived, and no one in that town or Maxville has seen her since.

Pax returns me to Missoula where I buy myself a pair of relaxed jeans that don't rub my leg wound so badly, a couple of clean shirts, one short sleeved one as it's reported to be hot as hell in New York City, and a pair of low heel boots easier to get on and off than my cowboy boots. It hurts like hell to pull them on and the first time I tried I was certain I'd popped some thigh stitches, from what's a very ugly wound, full of hematoma so it looks as if my leg's about to rot off.

I place a call to J. Cornelius Remington and, I'm not surprised, he's not in and not expected for a couple of months. A photo safari in Africa, with his daughter, so some officious woman informs me.

Bullshit.

So I buy a ticket and Pax puts me on a flight to Denver then New York City. I've stayed at the Waldorf, so this time I give the YMCA a try and a top bunk and common bath. In the shower in the morning a skinny kid with a chicken chest asks me, "You get shot up overseas or what."

"Nope, car wreck," I say, and it seems to satisfy him.

It's a hot muggy morning, with a flat gray ceiling that the Empire State pokes up into. The Upper East Side building with the discreet J. Remington Printers sign has a small parking garage next door. As the New York Giants' size doorman is already on duty, and can plainly see the entrance to the parking garage from his station near the door, I work my way to the back of the garage. With some difficulty I climb up on a garbage container the size of a Volkswagen, and jump the wall and am inside. On the third floor, next to a door that enters the building, is a parking space clearly marked J. Cornelius Remington. A car and a half away is a column next to the building, and it's just deep enough and dark enough that I can lean on the wall and wait out of sight of the slot, so I do.

It's forty five minutes with me reading a good mystery on my Kindle app on my iPhone when a tidy little refrigerator-white Porsche squeals the tires rounding the turns, then slides into the private parking space. Just peeking around the concrete, why am I not surprised to see J. Cornelius himself slip out of the little car, and why am I surprised to see Jane Jasper exit the passenger door?

They seem to be getting along famously and I don't quite let the building entry door close, and catch it, and follow them in. Realizing someone's behind them, both stop and turn.

"Good morning," I say, in my most pleasant tone.

Cornelius goes stark white, sucking air with his chin on his chest, but Jane Jasper attacks…in a good way, and flings her arms around me and hugs me so tightly I about have to scream out as she's got my arm wound under a half ton of pressure.

But she releases me and steps back, her eyes sparkling with excitment. "I'm so glad you're here and I get to thank you. They told me you brought us in. If it hadn't been for you...."

"I'm calling security," Cornelius manages.

I have my hand in the pocket of my loose jeans, simulating a gun, and give him a tight smile then suggest, "I wouldn't do that, J.C., if I was you." He goes even whiter, which I didn't think possible. So I continue. "What I would do is hit the button on that elevator and we're going up to your office to have a little chat."

Jane is looking back and forth from one of us to the other, then asks, "What's the matter, Daddy?"

I smile at her. "Can we go up. We need to talk over old times."

"Daddy, hit the button."

He does so, reluctantly. We exit, cross the outer office and enter his secretary's sanctuary. She looks up. "Good morning, Mr. Remington...Jane...and, why, look who's back."

I smile and nod and follow Remington into his office.

"Coffee?" the svelte good looking secretary calls after us.

"No," Remington snaps.

"I'd love some water," I call out and she smiles and shuts the door behind us. It was hot in the parking garage awaiting what I hope was worth waiting for.

As soon as the door closes, Remington rounds his desk but doesn't flop down in the chair. Instead, he leans forward, both hands fisted and leaning on the desktop. "You'd better leave, Reardon."

I turn to Jane. "Did you tell him what they tried to do to you?" I ask her.

"Why, yes, I told him they doped me up."
"And tried to burn you up?" I add.
"What do you mean?" she asks, puzzled.

Chapter Thirty Four

"Yes, burn you up. You didn't get the whole story?" I ask.

"What?" she replies.

"They had you three girls doped up and set the building on fire. You weren't supposed to get out. Pax..you don't know Pax..and I pulled you out."

Cornelius is indignant. "And how many people got killed in your little escapades?"

Jane looks at him with indignation that trumps his. "You call saving me an escapade?"

"That's not what I meant," he mumbles. "He's a violent man, with no thought of who gets hurt."

"Put your ass in that seat, Remington," I snap, and he does, like he's afraid I'm coming over the desk top. I turn to Jane, "And you take a seat also, please." And she does.

I begin unbuttoning my shirt.

"What..." he says, getting a little wide eyed.

"Shut up," I say, and pull the shirt off and unwrap an ace bandage from my arm, exposing the smaller of the wounds. He looks a little wide eyed, then gets even more so as I snap my NRA belt buckle loose, unbutton my jeans, and drop them to my ankles. Good thing I don't have holes in my boxer skivies.

"Now, see here..."

"Shut the fuck up, Conelius," I order, and begin unwrapping the ace bandage from my thigh. In moments, I've exposed that ugly puckered—now green, yellow, and purple—wound as well.

"I don't know what—"

"The what is you sent me into a battle and expected me to go in unarmed? This is the result of going in...and had I gone in unarmed, you wouldn't owe me the million four as I'd be full of embalming fluid. Those are bullet wounds you're seeing. Your sweet little girl is back here safe, per our agreement. So I'd suggest you pay up."

Just as I finish the sentence, his office door opens and the svelte secretary enters, my bottle of cold water in hand. She stops short, smiles as she looks me up and down, jeans resting on the top of my boots, and stammers, "Am I missing the party?"

"Get out," Remington snaps as she places the bottle on a coaster in front of me, her eyes sweeping me again, and with a broad smile she exits.

Jane cuts her eyes from my eyes, to my crotch, to her father. Her jaw clamped, speaking through her teeth she asks, "Did you promise to pay him, Daddy?"

"We talked about it—"

"No," I snap, re-wrapping the ace bandage on my leg. "We didn't talk about it, we shook hands on my returning your daughter, and my receiving twenty percent of the amount of her trust fund for doing so. You wanted your attorneys to draw up a contract. I said no, that you're a smart man...too smart to cross a man like me. Now do you remember?"

"You didn't return her. She came on her own volition."

"After I dragged her and two of her friends out of a fire. After I went after the asshole who coerced her to pay him and tried to turn her into a bucket of ashes. I'd understand your reluctance to pay up if I poured her out all over your desk and you had to take her home in an urn."

"Arne didn't actually coerce," Jane says, a little sheepishly.

"I shot Arne over his right eye so he won't be testifying for my success or failure. For whatever reason," I say, the most gentle way I can present my case. "You were there and under Arne's persuasion, and you were paying him lots of money. Most of which he was putting in offshore accounts, along with money he was getting from three or four other girls. Then he tried to barbecue you, Inga, and some redhead."

"I'm not paying," Cornelius growls. "She came home on her own."

I merely smile at him. "As you wish, Mr. Remington. But I'll tell you that you should find a good chiropractor."

"Why, I'm fine, thank you."

"Now, maybe. But you're gonna have a very sore neck from looking over your shoulder. I hate drug dealers, I hate human trafficers, I hate thieves of any kind and most of all I hate welching rats who don't do what they say. That would be you, Cornelius."

"Pay him, Daddy. I wouldn't be here were it not for him."

"Pay him, Daddy," I repeat. "Or you may never get another good night's sleep, for one time in the not so near future you'll wake up and I'll be standing at the foot of your beddy bye…maybe with my own can of high octane."

That makes his eyes widen. Then he murmurs, "How about the four hundred thousand we talked about?"

"*We* never talked about it, *you* talked about it. Pay up, one million four hundred thousand dollars in good old American greenbacks."

Jane stands and moves shoulder to shoulder with me, and glares at her old man. "If you don't pay him, I will, fifty thousand dollars every month, plus interest."

I flash her a smile. "At least one of the Remington family is a stand up dude."

Cornelius clamps his jaw so hard I'm surprised he doesn't bust teeth, and he actually stomps a foot, then shouts, "All right, God damn it. All right. If he'll just get the hell out of my office."

"Call your bank," I suggest. "I'll wait right here until the money arrives. Nice packets of hundreds will do. Then I'll be happy to have us part friends."

He grabs the phone, and I relax in my chair and sip my water while he makes the call, then gets up and stomps to the window and folds his hands in the small of his back. He glares at the great view.

Jane smiles at me. "You're not leaving right away are you?" she asks, then bats her eyes like the schoolgirl I hope she'll become again.

"I'll be happy to buy you dinner," I say.

"No you won't. I'm buying. I know this great little vegan—"

"No way. You can get French fries and spinach at Daddy's favorite, the Homestead."

Epilogue

Pax picks me up at the airport with a sunburn and a big smile. He's been flyfishing while I collected our money. He's happy with the quarter mil I give him, and Hunter, who's still in the hospital, is a little astounded when I tell him where in his backyard he can dig up the seventy-five grand I'm paying him for his trouble. I figure twenty five grand for his leg, same for his arm, same for his spleen, which is now in the hospital incinerator. I also put fifty grand on deposit for his hospital bill which should cover it and only proves how guilty I feel for leaving him to the wolves.

Pax and I fish the Bitterroot, Rock Creek, the Madison, the Jefferson, and finish on the Big Hole, and in a week are about ready to leave Montana for now very, very hot Las Vegas. Then I get a call from an unknown caller.

Inga. She must have gotten my number from Jane Jasper or Al at the bar.

"Hutchins bailed," she informs me.

"You're kidding?"

"No, I'm not. The judge set a half million and he got some guy in Helena—"

"Isenberg?"

"That's the guy. Treasure State Bail Bonds. Anyway, he's out, and I'm scared. I agreed to testify."

"You got an aunt in Pittsburgh or someplace you can go visit until the trial date?"

"No. And he'll never show up for the trial. He'll run for it."

"Good, then I can go after him."

"Where are you?" she asks, and I can hear the desperation in her voice.

"Over in the Big Hole. We're spending the night in Dillion then driving straight through to Vegas."

"Please, please, can I go with you?"

Who am I to turn down a request from a beautiful, tan, long-legged blond?

The hell of it is, a gentleman can't take advantage of a desperate woman. I'll have to wait until she's settled in a new job, and probably with a new identity before my conscious is clear and we're on even ground. So I'll work very hard finding her a good job in Vegas, a car, a place to live, and some confidence.

She says don't bother to drive back to Missoula, where she's hiding out, but that she'll ride the morning dog, the Greyhound, to Dillion.

"You heard about the stash?"

"What stash?" I ask.

"The sheriff, that cowboy from Phillipsberg, got a warrant and searched our cabin...I guess I should say Rostov's cabin...and found all the stuff he stole from Funky Furs under the floorboards. They lost a son, but at least they get most of their money back."

"Did he find anything else?"

"Not that I know of."

"See you in the morning, in Dillion."

173

"Thanks, Mike."

She has no idea how much it's my pleasure. Now if I can keep my horndog buddy, Pax, from beating my time.

As soon as she hangs up, I call the Granite County Sheriff's office, and the sheriff is in. "Sheriff Petersen. How's it with the county mounty?"

"If it isn't the mad motorcycle man, Mike Reardon."

"I'm complimented you recognize my voice."

"Who could miss a nice baritone like yours?"

"I understand you recovered some goods from Rostov's cabin?"

"I did, matching the description of the stuff stolen from Funky Furs."

"Anything else of interest?"

"Nope, that's enough."

I laugh. "Not quite enough. Wander up the south hill beyond the camp, about a hundred yards or so and you'll come across a nice crop. You do have a weed district in your county?"

"You bet. A real active one."

"Well, this weed may not qualify for one of their grants, but I'll bet you'll want to irradicate it none-the-less."

"The hell you say."

"I'll bet there're five hundred or maybe even a thousand plants."

"Why, thank you, Mike. That'll be a feather in my cap."

"Okay. See you around."

"You come on back anytime, ya hear. Hell, I'll even take you elk hunting."

"Sounds like a winner to me."

I hit the disconnect and turn to Pax. "Dillion?"

"Sure, I've caught and released two hundred pounds of fish. I'm ready for a steak."

"Okay. Hey, I got a bet for you, pretty boy."

"Oh yeah, what's that?"

"I'll bet that before we leave Dillion I can pick up a much better looking woman than you can. Mine'll make anything you drag in look like a skank."

"And you won't flash that sack of hundreds you're carrying?" He's very condescending, thinking I'd use money for such a thing.

"No, sir. No money involved. Besides, you got a full sack yourself. A hundred bucks suit you?"

"Suits me fine, dickwad. There's a first for everything."

I smile. I got him this time.

Here's a look at the next Mike Reardon, The Repairman novel, TARGET SHY & SEXY

Target Shy & Sexy

Prologue

No one could have been more surprised, after returning from a very tough job in Montana which ended in a week's fly fishing with my buddy—which wasn't so tough—to find a call waiting from a former employer.

Tammy Houston, rapidly becoming a very famous, very successful, country and western singer.

The hell of it is, the last time I did a gig for Tammy she fired me and it cost me fourteen grand to pay for the medical bills of a couple of young eco-terrorists who tried to defend a smartass kid who threw paint on what she thought was a fur coat. One lousy broken arm, only a slightly broken jaw, and the assholes deserved it. So I was out lots of dough and a month doing community service in a Seattle soup kitchen.

I'd snatched the wrist of the hippy girl who'd just thrown paint on Tammy's fur coat. The hell of it was the coat was faux fur and not that expensive. That didn't keep me from turning the young lady—if you can call a rude young hippy girl a lady—over my knee, right outside the Gaucho restaurant on 2nd Street in downtown Seattle, and tanning her butt until she bawled like a baby.

Of course I spent the night in the hoosegow...not for the spanking, but for breaking the jaw of one long-hair and the arm of another who decided to come to the property-destroying hippy girl's rescue. I take umbrage when someone is stupid enough to pull a two-inch blade penknife on me and broke that one's arm to cure him of said stupidity, and the jaw of the other as he called me a son-of-a-bitch and a cocksucker and tried to kick me in the gonads. Son-of-a-bitch I don't mind so much as I'm sure he was not really casting dispersions on my mom. My nads? Now that's another matter altogether. And a cocksucker? Now I take real umbrage at that. It was clearly a case of self-defense, however Judge Polkinghorn, who I'd like to poke in the eye, didn't agree.

It doesn't pay to beat up on rich-kid-liberals in Seattle; particularly when one's daddy is on the city council.

No good deed goes unpunished.

I also paid a five thousand dollar fine and did four weeks community service in a Seattle soup kitchen serving goulash to guys who drove up in BMW's. Truthfully not all of them drove up in anything, as many actually needed a hot meal. Having never begged, I'm not positive, but suspect it's much easier to work for a living.

I even made a few new friends while on the job, including a priest, Father Sean O'Donnel, who runs the joint. I traded some carpentry work—hanging doors—for a basement room while I paid my penance. I could have afforded a nearby hotel room, but one adds to life's experiences as one can...and I did.

As it turned out the judge did me a favor with the community service as I recognized a guy for whom I was dishing up some slop; a guy who'd skipped a hundred grand bail in Las Vegas. I called the bondsman, got a contract, put the guy facedown on the sidewalk after his next bummed bowl of soup and collected a twenty grand recovery fee for hauling him into the same lockup I'd recently left.

God works in mysterious ways.

Tammy still owes me for that week's work. I was not holding my breath waiting to collect, however it seems I'm now in demand. And she's a little more interested in my specialties, as someone knocked a great big chunk out of her fireplace in the multi million dollar condo she now occupies. Cops said a 50 cal mag did the deed.

The long-hairs' medical bills cost me fourteen thousand, so, after my three grand premium to a local bondsman, the fine, a few expenses, and the medical bills, I came out about three grand in the hole.

Living in the basement of a homeless shelter was not such a bad gig, as my primary residence, my second home, and my third and fourth are ministorage rooms…or at least had been until I invested in a 250 Ford truck and a camper. I also own a van, which is a necessity for the occasional bail enforcement—bounty hunting—I do. One occasionally needs tie downs and room to hook up a perp or two.

Of course I have an iPhone, and a half dozen throw away phones, so I really didn't need to drop by my buddy Pax Weatherwax's office. But he does have the best coffee in town, and the price is right.

Pax owns an Internet Service Provider company with offices in six cities, and keeps me out of trouble and loaded with information on clients and bad guys. Information that is probably just short of what the NSA could procure. He's really, really, really good at what he does.

And he's also my best friend, as we rambled through Desert Storm together, kept each other alive, and would have thrown ourselves on a grenade to save the other, if need be. As it is, he has one leg an inch shorter than the other thanks to dragging me out of a street singing with AK47 rounds and taking one through the thigh.

He still is the best man with a .308 I know—Marine sniper trained—and damn good with any other weapon. I don't want him after me, short leg or no.

I take the stairs up the back way to his two car garage size office, his back looking at the Vegas strip a few blocks distant, and catch him with his nose in some software manual.

"Hey!" I shout, and he jumps a foot.

"You son of a bitch," he stammers.

"Watch your mouth, fat boy," I say with a laugh.

"Fuck you. I can take you in anything but a foot race."

"I need to use a phone and want to put my butt in an easy chair to do so."

"Good, I'm busy here."

So I plop down in a far corner, grab the phone, and dial the area code 310 number Tammy left.

"Miss Houston's residence," the male voice answers.

"Funny, that's who I called." I'm feeling a little sassy as she's had to phone me, and I know it grates at her.

"May I say who's calling?"

"Mr. Michael Reardon, you may say."

"Is she expecting you?" he asks, his voice slightly more gruff.

"She might be expecting twins for all I know. I'm returning her call."

"You're a little flippant." His voice is even more gruff.

"You've got one minute to get her on the phone, or I'm hanging up. One more time, Sherlock, I'm returning her call."

"Right, hold on." I know he's put a hand over the receiver, but can hear him none-the-less. "Some smartass says he's returning your call. Michael Reardon."

It's far less than five seconds when she picks up the phone, and she's slightly out of breath like she's run to grab it.

"Hi, Mike."

"Hi, Miss Houston," I say, slightly tongue in cheek.

"You know its Tammy to you."

"Okay, Tammy. So long as I'm not working for you, it's Tammy. What's up?"

"I need your help."

I have to chuckle a little. "As I recall, you don't like my help."

"That was when I was young and naive. I've learned some things."

"Two years ago you were naïve and now your mature?"

"I've learned a lot."

"Okay," I sigh. "What do you need?"

"Protection. I'll explain it when you get here."

"Hell, there are a thousand guys out there—"

"I want you."

"You owe me for a week's work. You dropped me in the grease and cost me twenty grand."

"So, I was paying you five grand a week and cost you twenty grand, so a twenty five thousand retainer will get you back to work."

"Hardly. That's what you owe me. I now get ten grand a week for my services and require a two week retainer."

"Ten grand...who do you think you are? Merle Haggard?"

"Nope, I've never done time in the big house."

She's quiet for a moment, then, "So, twenty thousand will get you here?"

"Plus the twenty five grand you owe me."

"You drive a tough bargain."

"And I'm very tough on people who mean to do my clients harm. And if Forbes knows, you're knocking down five mil a month and that alone will attract some scumbags."

"Yeah, but I have a lot of expenses." She's silent for a moment. "Will you be at this number? I've got it on my phone here."

"I'll be here until I take a buddy to supper. Maybe an hour or so."

"I'll call you back."

"Whatever," I say. I saw that in some hot shot young Hollywood movie, so I guess it's the thing to say to twenty five year olds.

"I'll call. I've got to clear it with Emory."

"Whatever....or maybe I should say, whomever." There, I've said it twice. Am I hip, or what?

So I hang up. It's good to have money in the bank and be independent.

She calls back in fifteen minutes, with an affirmative.

Chapter One

I'd returned Tammy's call on a Friday and she asked me to be front and center at her condo in Beverly Hills at 9:00 AM on Monday morning to meet with her manager, Emory, and get up to speed on the job. He was to have a check for me in the amount of forty-five grand, the twenty-five she'd cost me and the twenty grand retainer.

Not as bad as Sunday night, still Monday morning is a terrible time to drive from Vegas to L.A., as you're taking your life in your hands with the last of the weekend traffic. Those folks may have knocked down the free booze at the tables right up until they climbed in their SUV's and headed for the City of the Angels. So I climb in my Vette at three AM. The drunks are still on the highway, but fewer of them and you have a little room to duck and dodge. As I'm not applying for a job at IBM I wear a soft brown pullover, black Wranglers, and black Rebocs...when Tammy was young, two years ago, she required her security to be in coat and tie. So we looked like security. I hope she's outgrown that affectation.

The condo is in a high rise—at least twenty stories—on Wilshire in Westwood. I guess Tammy thinks Beverly Hills sounds more prestigious, and, after all, it's only a stones throw. I guess the condo building at twenty stories as Tammy's address is No. 2001. With, of course, a three hundred pound guard at the entrance to the parking garage. He informs me that he does not have me on a visitor list, so "...please back it up and let me see your tail as you disappear." He's a real card. I find a place on the street three blocks away, and call the number Tammy had left for me earlier.

No answer.

I'm not anal about much, but being on time...in fact doing what I say I'm going to do...is on top the list.

The entry to the building is lined with video cameras, and like the garage there's an attendant, a doorman behind a counter in the foyer. The foyer is marble—floor and walls—and the ceiling is brass with tiny inset LED lighting. There's a ten by ten foot brass relief of a number of old stars—Bing Crosby, Elvis, Sinatra, Al Jolson, and others—on one wall and the face of the counter and the counter itself is brass. There's one bench, uncomfortable cold marble, for those asked to wait.

I'm not surprised to find the large glass door locked and a video camera and press-to-talk box on the wall nearby. When I try the door, no neck, the guard, points at the brass box so I comply.

"Here to see Tammy Houston's people, have an appointment. I'm Mike Reardon."

Without looking at a calendar, he replies. "I have you on the calendar." And buzzes me in.

As I head for the elevator, he adds. "I don't think there's anyone up there. You a cop?"

Where'd he get that? I glance down at the way I'm dressed, brown shirt and all, and say with all seriousness, "Undercover with UPS."

He nods. I guess there's no IQ test for doorman/guard.

It's a fast elevator to the penthouse floor, where I observe as I step out, there are only two penthouse apartments. Tammy's wasting no time blowing her five mil a month. I guess she's never studied the phrase, fame is fleeting.

Maybe already flown.

Door with 2001 in brass letters has yellow crime tape strung across the opening.

Neither the parking garage attendant nor the doorman mentioned the fact the place was sealed up...but that explains the doorman asking if I was a cop.

None the less, I ring the bell and can hear the notes to Tammy's first big hit, *Houston Hottie* in lieu of the standard two tone.

No one answers. Which does not surprise me as cops don't normally seal someone inside a crime scene.

Not to be easily dissuaded I return to the copper accented foyer and as I leave wave my phone at the guard. "I'm ten minutes early. The detective said he'd be a little late. I'll be right back."

My well-worn lock pick set and rubber gloves are in the Vette. These days fingerprints are less important as there are probably a half dozen video cameras trained on me between my parking spot and the building, and some real good closeups taken from front door and foyer cameras, and as I felt no need I've not employed any facial disguise. Still, I don't want the absolute proof of prints left at the scene.

No, I don't think my check will be waiting on a kitchen counter, but I do want to see what the hell's up. This time the door guard buzzes me in as I top the entry stairs.

I'm operating on the premise that the "do not enter" on the crime scene tape is advice, not an order. And, after all, I've been invited by the owner occupant.

It takes me all of thirty seconds to pop the entry lock, and another full minute on the dead bolt. It takes longer to work my way through the crisscross crime scene tape without ripping it off the jamb.

The condo is at least six thousand square feet with living room, kitchen, expansive dinning room, powder room, two guest rooms with baths, and a patio larger than the average city apartment on the entry floor and a winding stairway to a second floor. I do find the chunk out of the fireplace, which was the reason I was called in the first instance. If it came through the sliding glass door leading out to the patio, it's been repaired. After seeing nothing else out of order on that floor, I ascend the stairway to a balcony with four doors, one of which is a double door and I presume the master.

And I'm right as I enter to see a bed about the size of a soccer field.

Opposite the headboard is a floor-to-ceiling window wall, and I quickly spot the reason for the crime scene tape.

The bad news: a perfect bullet hole head high in the glass, with cracks spider-webbing out at least a foot all around. Someone was serious, as it, again, appears to be a fifty caliber.

Am I too late to protect Miss Houston? I have to consciously relax my jaw as my teeth are beginning to ache. No matter how young and ignorant Tammy had been during our first mutual experience, I liked her and would hate to think of her shot by some Neanderthal stalker...or anyone else for that matter.

The good news: no bloodstains anywhere in the bedroom.

The ceiling is at least ten feet high, and the first thing I look for is a bullet hole in the opposite wall, and it's not hard to locate as it's near the ceiling next to the bed, with an orange felt-tip-pen circle around where a bullet's been dug out of the wall by some CSI dude.

So the shot came at an upward angle, as is not surprising firing at a twenty storey condo. Even though there are a half dozen other buildings within a half mile of the condo, it's fairly simple to determine the likelihood of where the shot came from and I note the location of a twelve to fifteen storey building a few hundred yards to the west, also fronting on Wilshire Boulevard. It's rooftop is a couple of stories lower than Tammy's building, thus the up angle.

There's no question in my mind that LAPD or whoever is the "power that be" in Westwood has worked the building from which the shot obviously came, so I don't bother creeping that location.

It's more important to discover what happened to Tammy.

And to have breakfast.

Every once in a while I splurge with calories, and I know a spot close by. Mon Amour Café is only a couple of blocks and has crepes that will break even an old country boy who loves flapjacks into a cold sweat. I grab an *L.A. Times* on the way in and am only two bites into their 'original crepe' that comes with bananas and strawberries, slathered with whipped cream, when I find an article in the local section. "Country Star Houston Flees Attempted Murder." The article goes on to say after a gunshot was fired into her condo, she disappeared into the night with her entourage. The cops have no clue who tried to drop our diva.

After dusting off the original for breakfast and a chocolate one for dessert, I am ready to get to work. Don't go to this joint for service, only if you love crepes and can stand creeps.

Once settled back in my Vette, I call my buddy Pax in Vegas.

"Hey, I need a little keyboard magic."

"Make it quick, I'm busy."

"Do I need to find a new best friend?"

"Fuck you, Farley. Ask."

"Somebody tried to dust my new client before she becomes my new client. See what you can find out about what happened and to where she might have flown. She's hiding out and not answering the number I have. You might try her manager for a phone number, some guy named Emory something."

"I'll put Sol on it. He can be your next best friend."

"Good, he's better than you anyway."

"Sit on it, Sunshine."

"I'll stand by."

I read the rest of my paper, and it's a good thing I read fast as my phone buzzes and it's Sol, who's one of those twenty five year old computer genius types who's worked for Pax since he was a teenager.

"She has a place in Malibu." He gives me an address near Point Dume State Park. "The land line there is unlisted but it's 555-6720."

"Also 310, right."

"Right. And her manager, Emory Coogan, is 805-555-3433."

"I owe you a tall cold one."

"How about a five foot two blonde one."

"Drinks I can do, Sol. You got to take care of your own love life."

"But you're so much better at it."

"You're in Vegas, my man. A blonde on every street corner."

"Yeah, but I don't pay for it."

"Thanks for the help."

"*De nada.*"

So I dial the Malibu land line. No answer, get a machine, and leave a message. So I dial Coogan and likewise get a recording and leave a message.

I can be there in thirty minutes, traffic allowing, so head out. It's a great drive and a great day, so I put the top down on the Vette and enjoy it.

Nothing like a drive up the California coast on a beautiful day with an ocean breeze and California King Gulls circling overhead.

And I'm happy, until I work my way through the maze of roads at Dume Point and arrive at Tammy's ocean front address…and there's yellow crime scene tape strung all over the driveway.

A half-dozen L.A. County sheriff cars.

An ambulance.

What the hell?

About the Author

L. J. Martin is the author of more than three dozen works of both fiction and non-fiction from Bantam, Avon, Pinnacle and his own Wolfpack Publishing. He lives in Montana wtih his wife, NYT bestselling romantic suspense author Kat Martin. He's been a horse wrangler, cook as both avocation and vocation, volunteer firefighter, real estate broker, general contractor, appraiser, disaster evaluator for FEMA, and traveled a good part of the world, some in his own ketch. A hunter, fisherman, photographer, cook, father and grandfather, he's been car and plane wrecked, visited a number of jusgados and a road camp, and survived cancer twice. He carries a bail-enforcement shield. He knows about what he writes about.

For more great action-adventure novels from acclaimed author L. J. Martin go to:

www.ljmartin.com
(click on the title or the cover to go to a purchase link)

18636693R00112

Made in the USA
Middletown, DE
17 March 2015